THE SECRET OF SKULL MOUNTAIN

THERE is a crisis in Bayport! Soon the city will be without water! Every night water strangely disappears from the new reservoir near Skull Mountain. Frank and Joe Hardy join forces with a team of skilled engineers to solve the baffling mystery.

When the boys arrive at the foot of the mountain, they are met by a human skull rolling down the slope—a chilling warning from a weird hermit. Violence, too, stalks the mountain, where a gang controlled by a powerful crime syndicate hatches a vicious plot. While trying to uncover the gang's sinister motive, Frank and Joe aid their detective father in his search for a missing scientist.

By a clever experiment, the boys discover a clue to the puzzle of the vanishing water. Suspense mounts when they explore an ancient subterranean river channel, deep inside Skull Mountain. In a thrilling climax the famous young detectives solve their own mystery as well as Mr. Hardy's case.

"Watch out!" Joe yelled. "He's going to throw it!"

Hardy Boys Mystery Stories

The SECRET of SKULL MOUNTAIN

BY

FRANKLIN W. DIXON

NEW YORK
GROSSET & DUNLAP
Publishers

CONTENTS

CHAPTER I

A Mysterious Skull

"WHAT do you mean, we can't go swimming?"
asked Joe Hardy.

"Not in the Bayport pool," said Frank, who
was at the wheel of their convertible.

"You're kidding!"

"No, I'm not," replied the tall, dark-haired
boy. "There isn't enough water. The shortage is
getting serious."

Joe, blond and seventeen, and a year younger
than Frank, glanced at his watch and flipped the
radio switch. It was news time. The suave voice
of the broadcaster came in clearly.

"City officials announced today that unless a
way is found to fill Tarnack Reservoir, the people of Bayport may soon be without water. Thou-
sands of gallons flow in daily from the river, but
overnight the water vanishes."

"That's strange," said Joe. "Why should it—" He broke off as the announcer went on:

"Robert Carpenter, a local engineer, has been employed by the builders of the dam to find out why the reservoir is not filling properly, but so far he has failed to provide a solution—"

"Carpenter," Frank mused as he turned down the volume. "He's a fine engineer. Must be a tough problem if he can't find the answer."

"Yes," Joe agreed. "I'm— Frank! Look out!"

Frank had not noticed the tall young man who had stepped absent-mindedly from the curb. He was reading a newspaper and walking directly into the path of the car!

At Joe's warning, Frank twisted the wheel and jammed on the brakes. The car screeched to a halt, but the bumper caught the pedestrian and knocked him down. The boys jumped out and ran to the man.

"Dick Ames!" Joe exclaimed.

"Dick," Frank asked anxiously, "are you hurt?"

Their friend sat up and wiped his forehead with a handkerchief. "No," he replied. Then, recognizing the boys, he gave a weak grin. "Thanks to you!" He took a deep breath. "That was dumb of me to jaywalk while reading. But I was so angry about this reservoir story I forgot to watch where I was going."

The boys helped the tall, good-looking young man to his feet.

"We'll give you a lift," said Frank. "Where you going?"

"To my parking garage."

Dick got into the convertible between the brothers and Frank drove on, past the curious motorists who had stopped to see the accident.

"My car's at the Midtown Garage," Dick said. "You can drop me there."

"You okay?" Joe asked, noting his pale face.

"I'm okay—just sore about this story," said Dick, slapping the newspaper. "The reporters aren't giving us a chance!"

"Are you working on the mystery?" Frank asked.

"Yes. I'm Bob Carpenter's assistant—" Dick broke off and stared at the boys suspiciously. "Who told you it's a mystery?"

Frank grinned as Joe gave him a sly wink. "It doesn't take a detective long to figure out that when a reservoir won't fill, and an engineer with Mr. Carpenter's reputation can't find the reason for it, something mysterious is going on," Frank said.

The Hardy boys' interest in mysteries was well known in Bayport. Their father, Fenton Hardy, was one of the finest private detectives in the United States. Frank and Joe, although still in high school, had helped him solve many baffling cases. Their most recent one had been the mystery of *The Phantom Freighter*.

The boys proceeded to question Dick eagerly about the disappearing water.

The engineer frowned. "I can't figure it. Last week, work was completed on the dam to impound the Tarnack River, and also on the conduit which is to carry the water to Bayport. The entire construction was inspected and passed A-OK."

"Then why is the water running out?"

"You tell me," said Dick. "All I know is it's not a simple leak. There's something weird about the whole problem."

"What do you mean?" Frank asked.

Dick cast him an odd glance. "You fellows know Skull Mountain?"

"Just that the dam and reservoir are there," Frank replied.

"It's a rugged place," said Dick, "covered with dark woods. Strange things have been happening there. Spooky, if you ask me."

"You think somebody's trying to scare you off?"

"Yes. That's what makes me feel sure there's skulduggery connected with the loss of the water. Besides, why does it only disappear at night?"

Silently the boys pondered the problem as Frank threaded the car through downtown traffic. Suddenly Joe noticed that their passenger had become very pale.

"What's the matter, Dick?"

"I'm sorry, fellows. I guess that bump shook me up a little, after all."

"You're coming home with us," Joe said. "You can lie down, and if that doesn't cure you," he added, grinning, "Aunt Gertrude will stuff you to the ears with the best food you've ever tasted."

Supper was on the table when Frank and Joe arrived home with Dick Ames. Both Mrs. Hardy and Aunt Gertrude met them at the door, and Frank told what had happened.

Mrs. Hardy was concerned about Dick and wanted him to lie down at once.

But Aunt Gertrude would not hear of it. "Fiddlesticks!" she scoffed. "The boy's just shaken up. There's nothing wrong with Dick that a plate of sausage and waffles won't fix!"

Dick surprised them by agreeing. The fresh air during the drive to the house had made him feel better and the aroma of frying sausage was giving him a ravenous appetite.

Aunt Gertrude's smile was so triumphant that Frank and Joe could not help laughing. Their aunt looked at them suspiciously.

"What are you two chortling about?" she demanded. "Hurry up and set a place for Dick!"

Aunt Gertrude lived at the home of her brother, Fenton Hardy. Despite her tart manner, she was very fond of Frank and Joe, and proud of their success as amateur sleuths.

As the three boys sat down to large servings of

sausage and waffles, they learned that Mrs. Hardy and Aunt Gertrude already knew about the threatened water shortage. A radio announcer had described the situation and urged listeners to limit their use of water.

"Humph!" Aunt Gertrude sniffed. "What does he think we've been doing all these years?" She speared another piece of sausage with her fork. "The authorities of this city should be ashamed of themselves. Pass the syrup, Frank. Why, even five years ago Bayport didn't have enough water. Joe, don't eat so fast. The whole city might burn down any time. And what's more, how will we cook without water?" she finished.

"Wow!" Frank laughed. "We'll have to do something." He looked across the table at their guest. "Dick, think Mr. Carpenter could use a couple of sleuths to help him find out why the reservoir won't fill?" He glanced hopefully at Joe.

Dick paused. "He might at that," he said slowly. "Maybe you can find out what the trouble is on Skull Mountain. How soon could you come?"

"Right away!" the boys chorused.

"Swell!" Dick said. "I must get back to the camp this evening. We'll drive out there together now. It's about twenty miles. Plan to stay over."

"You can leave your car at the garage," said Frank. "We'll take ours."

"None of you are going anywhere until you've had your dessert," Aunt Gertrude put in firmly. "Apple cake."

"Why, Aunty!" Joe grinned and winked at Frank. "The biggest mystery in the world couldn't tear us away until we'd eaten your apple cake!"

An hour later Frank was driving along the highway toward Skull Mountain, with Joe and Dick beside him. Packed in the trunk were pup tents and cots, hiking clothes and other camping equipment, as well as a basket of sandwiches and cake Mrs. Hardy and Aunt Gertrude had prepared. Joe was wearing a pair of powerful field glasses on a lanyard around his neck.

"You two must be real chow-hounds," Dick said with a grin. "Bob and I have food at camp. You didn't need to bring your own."

Frank laughed. "You don't know Aunt Gertrude. She wouldn't have let us out of the house without that basket."

After a while they saw a cluster of low mountains in the distance. To reach them, Frank turned off the highway onto a narrow dirt road. On their right loomed Skull Mountain.

Joe gave a low whistle. "It looks spooky all right!"

The mountain was a high, dark, forbidding mass. Although it was thickly covered with trees,

the slope just above the road was scarred by stretches of jagged rock and huge boulders. Few people in the area ever undertook the hazardous climb to the summit.

Suddenly Joe gripped Frank's arm. "Look!" he cried out. "A fire! It might be a forest fire!"

Frank braked the car as Joe whipped the field glasses from their case. The boys and Dick Ames piled out of the car and Joe trained the binoculars on the mountaintop. A thin column of smoke rose from the trees which obscured the crest of the hill, then drifted across the valley.

"It's not a forest fire," said Dick. "We've seen it before."

"What is it then?" Frank asked. "Somebody living up there?"

"I don't know and neither does Bob Carpenter!" Dick answered. "We have a hunch the smoke is connected somehow to the trouble at the reservoir."

Joe started toward the slope. "Come on! Let's look for that fire now!"

"Hold it," said Dick. "I know a trail we can use. We'll make better time."

The boys hurried down the road in the direction they had come, keeping an eye on the curling smoke. The path Dick showed them led up the mountain through the low brush toward masses of boulders near the top.

They climbed rapidly, glancing often at the summit.

As suddenly as it had arisen, the smoke vanished. "Now you see it, now you don't!" exclaimed Joe.

"Let me have a look," Frank suggested. He focused the field glasses on the spot where they had seen the smoke. "Nothing in sight now."

Frank turned slowly, examining the mountainside. Suddenly, from behind a boulder, appeared one of the strangest-looking figures he had ever seen. The man was gaunt-faced, with fierce-looking eyes, long shaggy hair, and a thick beard. Frank uttered a low exclamation.

"What's wrong?" Joe demanded.

"Look at that funny guy up there," Frank said, handing his brother the glasses.

Joe trained the binoculars on the boulder Frank indicated, but saw no sign of the bearded man. Disappointed, he gave the glasses to Dick, but the young engineer could not detect him either.

"What did he look like, Frank?" Dick asked as they turned back toward the car.

Frank described the man, but the engineer shook his head and declared that although he had met some odd people on Skull Mountain, none of them matched the description.

As the three started down the hill, a rounded white object rolled past them and lodged against a bush.

"A skull!" Joe exclaimed. As he picked it up, the trio heard an ominous rumbling. They faced about swiftly.

Hurtling down the slope was a huge boulder!

"Look out!" Frank shouted, and they leaped aside.

Crack! The boulder struck another and dislodged a mass of loose rock.

A rain of rocks and brush and boulders came roaring down around them!

"A landslide!" Joe yelled.

CHAPTER II

Strange Laughter

"Run!" Frank shouted.

Joe, Frank, and Dick Ames scrambled to get out of the path of the thundering mass of rocks. Minutes later the landslide roared into silence below and dust filled the air.

Coughing, Joe got to his feet. "Frank—Dick!" he called and was relieved to hear answering voices.

The three met where the trail had been, now a wide, raw strip of earth, scoured clean of rocks and brush.

"Whew!" Joe exclaimed. "That was close." He was so shaken he did not notice that he was still clutching the skull.

"That's the second time today my life's been in danger," Dick said. "Must be the season for accidents."

Frank shook his head angrily. "That was no accident, Dick. I'm pretty sure that our man of the mountain caused the landslide. The first big boulder looked like the one he had been hiding behind."

Joe's lips tightened. "I'm going after that guy!"

"Wait, Joe!" Frank said. "It's no use. Soon it'll be dark. We'd better push on to camp."

Joe looked down at the skull in his hand. "I wonder if our mountain man rolled this down, too."

Dick looked grim. "That's not the first one I've seen around here, and I'll bet it's not the last."

Joe grinned. "Well, Bony doesn't look much like a good-luck charm, but why don't we appoint him mascot for our new mystery?"

When the boys reached the car, they propped the skull on the dashboard and set out for the camp. After they had traveled another mile, Dick showed Frank a clearing where he could park.

"We'll have to hike from here," the engineer explained.

The three shouldered their camping equipment and started up a narrow, winding trail toward the top of the mountain.

For a time, they climbed steadily. Then the path grew steep and treacherous. Rockslides had blocked it in places, and at several points heavy rains had washed away large chunks of earth.

Finally Joe halted. "It's too steep!" he said. "I can't keep my footing unless I unload some of this gear—my pack's throwing me off balance."

"We'd better not leave anything here," Frank pointed out. "We haven't any equipment to spare."

"There must be an easier way to reach the reservoir," said Joe. "How did the dam-builders truck in supplies?"

"They cut a road up the other side of the mountain," Dick replied, "but it's not paved. We've had so much rain lately, I was afraid your car would stick in the mud."

"Let's try this way," Frank suggested, pointing to a narrow branch of the trail which sloped more gradually.

The alternate path proved to be easier climbing and soon they were standing on a crest overlooking Tarnack Valley.

"There it is!" Dick said, pointing downward. "Our big headache!"

Far below, through the gathering dusk, Frank and Joe could see the reservoir, a shimmering sheet of water behind a towering white concrete dam.

"You don't need to know much about engineering to know that's great," Frank remarked. "It's super."

"It must have been a tough job to build," Joe remarked as they started down toward the dam.

Dick explained that the Tarnack River had flowed over the valley bottom. "Its course had to be diverted before the engineers could construct the reservoir. When the dam was completed, the river was rediverted to its old bed."

Joe looked down at the dam in admiration. "So the river flows along the way it always has, and at the same time it does a whole new job!"

"It ought to work that way," Dick said. "We have to find out why it doesn't. Everything's set for the water to flow into Bayport. But we can't release it until we're sure we can maintain the proper level in the reservoir. So far, the water hasn't risen high enough.

"Right now, Bayport is being supplied by Upstate Reservoir, a hundred miles north of here. But so many towns have sprung up in this area that Upstate can no longer take care of us. Day by day the amount we get dwindles."

Dick told the boys that the dam had been built by the Coastal Power and Light Company. "When it's working, it will supply electricity to this whole region as well as water to Bayport. But so far it's a multimillion-dollar dud!"

Frank and Joe scanned the valley. Trees had been cleared from a point level with the top of the dam down to the water's edge. The high banks of the reservoir were covered with vines and low shrubs. There was one patch of high, thick bushes.

Frank knitted his brows. "That's odd!" he exclaimed. "Shouldn't all of those bushes have been cleared?"

The construction men did take out most of them," Dick replied. "But a few days before they were finished, they were caught in a rockslide."

"Anyone hurt?" Joe asked.

"Yes. Three of the men were seriously injured. Then the rest of the crew decided the job was too risky and laid down their tools. We'll have the job completed when the ground freezes and there is less danger of a landslide."

The three continued down the slope. The way was much easier now, and they moved rapidly. Soon they could see a small construction shack among the trees some distance above the reservoir.

Dick cupped his hands to his mouth and called down. Bob Carpenter came out of the shack. "Hi!" he replied as the others approached him. The engineer was tall and sun-tanned, with an intelligent face and a friendly manner. He studied Frank and Joe with keen interest as Dick introduced them.

"Hardy? You must be Fenton Hardy's sons."

"We are," said Frank.

"In that case, I'm twice as glad to see you," Bob Carpenter said, smiling. He shook their hands firmly and waved toward the shack. "Welcome to Carpenter's Cottage!"

The engineers led the way to the shack, and as the boys followed, they noted that it was sturdily built. Some distance to the rear was an equipment hut, a pile of sand, and one of lumber. Inside, Dick lit a kerosene lamp and gave Bob the evening newspaper.

Bob Carpenter's face grew grim as he read the story of the water shortage.

"This paper's pretty rough on me," he remarked. "If I don't lick this problem, boys, it could lick me. My professional reputation won't be worth a nickel!"

"You and Dick are not trying to do this job alone, are you?" asked Frank.

"No," replied Bob Carpenter. "I have a six-man work crew staying in a cabin over at the foot of the dam. They've been using electronic equipment to listen for a leak along the shores of the reservoir."

"But there's so much ground to cover," Dick put in, "that it'll take a long while."

"Maybe we can save you time by getting to the root of the trouble, Joe said. "Let us have a crack at the case."

"Dick says some strange things have been going on here," Frank said. "Tell us about them."

"Well, one strange thing is the smoke," Bob said, frowning. "A thin column of it rises from the top of the mountain every so often. We've searched carefully, but haven't found any sign of a fire."

"Dick told us about that. And we just saw the same smoke!" Frank said.

The youth related what had happened while he, Joe, and Dick were driving along the road at the foot of the mountain. Frank had hoped that Bob Carpenter would be able to identify the strange man of the mountain, but the engineer was perplexed.

Suddenly Frank felt a prickling at the back of his neck. He whirled and looked at the dark window behind him. *Had someone been peering into the shack?* "I'm going to take a look around outside," he said quietly.

"I'll go with you," Joe insisted.

Taking flashlights, they stepped outside. Darkness lay on the mountain with a light mist over the reservoir below. The boys separated and began circling the shack.

Suddenly Frank heard a scurrying sound and the crackle of twigs. He flashed his light, and saw a bush spring back in place. He ran to the spot, but saw no sign of anything moving.

"What was it?" Joe whispered as he came up to him.

Frank shrugged. "Maybe only an animal."

They went back into the shack.

"Find anything?" Bob asked.

Frank shook his head. "Who is on the mountain beside yourselves?"

"There are some squatters in this area," Bob replied, "but I never came across one who matches your description."

"Squatters?" Joe repeated.

"Yes," Dick said. "There were several squatters living in the valley when the contractors moved in to build the reservoir. Most of them gave up their homes and moved back over the ridge to the other side of the mountain. But two—Sailor Hawkins and Potato Annie—refused to leave and are still hanging onto their shacks on the mountainside."

"Would Sailor Hawkins or Potato Annie be likely to roll a boulder or toss a skull at us?" queried Frank.

Bob laughed. "I doubt it. They're troublesome, but I've no proof that they're the ones trying to scare me away from here."

Joe's interest quickened. "What do you mean—scare?"

Bob laughed again. "Well, I found a skull planted in my knapsack—and another on my worktable."

"Golly!" said Joe. "Where do they all come from?"

"Years ago Indians lived in the valley," Bob told them, "and their burial ground is somewhere on the mountain. Maybe the skulls come from there."

He said that tools had been stolen from the camp and surveying equipment had been smashed.

"Someone's mighty anxious to keep you from

finding out what's wrong with the reservoir," Joe remarked.

Bob nodded. "But they won't get rid of me. I'm not leaving till I know the answer to this puzzle."

"You can count on us, Mr. Carpenter," said Frank, and Joe nodded his agreement.

The engineer smiled. "Call me Bob." He glanced at his watch. "Now, let's hit the sack. We have plenty to do tomorrow!"

It was a half hour's work for the boys to set up their pup tents close by Carpenter's Cottage, and soon they were asleep in their cots.

Some time later Frank found himself wide awake. *Had that been a branch cracking outside the tent?* He lay quiet, listening. There it was again—farther away!

As he started to get up, there came a loud roar and the cot heaved. Frank was flung to the ground. *An explosion!* Debris thudded onto the tent! After that there was silence. Frank sat up, unhurt. Then, from some distance away, he heard a shrill cackling laugh!

CHAPTER III

Chet Joins Up

"FRANK!"

Joe's cry sent a chill of fear through his brother. The older boy crawled hurriedly out of his tent. A lot of the debris had fallen on Joe's tent and knocked it down. Joe was floundering under the canvas like an angry sea lion.

As Frank helped him crawl out, he saw Joe was not injured, though the tent was badly torn.

"Whew!" Joe exclaimed. "What happened?"

"You know as much as I do," Frank told him. "Put your shoes on and let's have a look."

The boys found their flashlights and joined Bob and Dick, who had come rushing out with a lantern.

It did not take them long to find the spot where the explosion had occurred. A huge jagged hole had been torn in the ground.

"It's a war of nerves," Bob said grimly. "Somebody hopes we'll crack under the strain and go away."

"I wish I could lay my hands on that guy," Joe said as they started back. "That cackle of his gave me the creeps."

Suddenly Frank stopped. On the ground, in the beam of his flashlight, were the prints of two naked human feet. The right one showed the small toe to be missing.

"You know anybody who goes around barefoot?" Frank asked Bob and Dick.

The engineers shook their heads.

"Maybe the old man of the mountain does," Frank said. "Joe and I will follow the prints first thing in the morning."

The sun was well up when the boys awoke to the aroma of frying bacon. Breakfast over, they set out to follow the prints, which led up the mountain.

In some places the tracks were barely distinguishable. In others, where the mud was soft, they were strikingly clear. After climbing for a while, Frank and Joe found themselves a stone's throw from a stretch of cleared land where row upon row of potato plants and other vegetables were growing. Behind the garden patch was a small shanty.

"That must be Potato Annie's place," Frank said.

"Yes," agreed Joe. "And the footprints are heading straight for it!"

As they approached the tidy garden, the boys saw a woman working in it. She wore a sunbonnet with an enormous peak that completely shaded her face, a faded cotton dress, and a huge checkered apron. Potato Annie was barelegged but she was wearing shoes. The boys noted that her feet were too small to have made the prints.

She straightened up at their approach and stared. "Who be you?" she demanded.

"We're from Mr. Carpenter's camp," Frank began, "and we—"

"Oh, you be, be you!" Annie cut him short. "Then you git on back there, if you know what's good fer you! Ain't no engineers goin' to traipse on my land!"

"We're not engineers," Joe tried to explain. "We're—"

But Potato Annie was adamant. "You hear me! Git! Good-fer-nothin' loafers—drivin' self-respectin' people off their property!" Then, as the boys turned away, the spry little woman demanded, "What you want?"

"We only came for some information, Frank told her. He described the column of smoke they had seen, and the explosion, but although Annie admitted she had seen the smoke and heard the explosion, she insisted that she did not know who was responsible.

"Have you ever come across any skulls around here?" Joe asked.

"Skulls?" scoffed the old woman. "Why, there's a million of 'em buried on the other side o' this mountain! That's how the place got its name. My grandpaw told me a whole Injun tribe is buried here!"

Frank tried another tack. "Did you ever see an old man on the mountain?" he asked. "A gaunt-faced fellow with long shaggy hair?"

A flicker of fear crossed Annie's face, but she declared flatly that she had never seen nor heard of such a creature. Frank thanked the old woman for her information.

"Ain't told you nothin', far as I know," she retorted. She watched the boys start down the slope from which they had come. "Tell them engineers this valley ain't never goin' to be covered with water!" she yelled after them. "Tell 'em Annie said so!"

The boys grinned at each other and looked back. Annie was bending over her potato plants again.

Frank's face grew sober. "She knows the mountain man."

Joe nodded. "Let's try to pick up the prints again outside her place and see where they go."

The boys slipped behind a clump of bushes

and watched the woman, waiting for her to go inside. Finally she squinted up at the sun, put down
her hoe, and went into the shack.

"Come on, Joe!"

Quickly they made their way to the small
farm and searched around it until they found the
bare footprints. For a while they were able to follow the trail up the mountain. Then the ground
became gravelly and the tracks vanished.

Hot and hungry, the boys returned to the
camp, where they had a late lunch of sandwiches
and milk. Afterward they walked down to the
reservoir. Men were working around the shore
with electronic devices, while the two engineers
slowly circled in a rowboat. Bob dropped white-
painted shingles in the water at regular intervals.

Frank waved, and Dick rowed the boat toward
them. A few yards from the shore he rested his
oars.

"What are you doing?" Joe asked.

"Trying to find out where the water is escaping," Bob explained. "The river is feeding the
reservoir, but the water won't rise over twenty
feet."

"The shingles will help us to detect currents
that may indicate a hidden outlet," Dick added.

Joe looked puzzled. "Why are you doing it
now? I thought it only emptied at night."

"That's when most of the run-off takes place,"
Dick replied, "but there might be a little drain-

age during the day. We're checking every possibility."

"You've had no luck at night?" Frank asked.

Bob scowled. "Every time we come down here after dark, somebody shoots at us with a high-powered rifle."

Frank raised his eyebrows. "A sniper."

"Several of them," Dick corrected him with a grimace. "We get cross fire."

"They've hit the boat twice," Bob put in, "and we've repaired it. Frankly, it's pretty risky. I've been trying to think of a safer way to investigate." Then he added, "What have you two been up to?"

Frank described how the trail of the footprints had led them to Potato Annie. Bob agreed that the woman could be in on the trouble.

"She will have to move, won't she?" Joe asked.

"As soon as the reservoir begins to function, she'll be forced off the land. This will be a restricted area."

Joe grinned. "I feel sorry for the fellows who have to make her go."

Frank reminded Joe that they had to drive to town to replace Joe's damaged tent. "We'll be back before nightfall," he told the engineers.

"Wait a minute," said Joe. The landslide—the road will be blocked."

"You can get out," said Dick. He told them of a fork in the dirt road which would take them to the highway.

An hour later when the Hardy boys drove up to their home, Aunt Gertrude was on the lawn, digging out dandelions. Joe, his eyes twinkling, picked up the skull from the dashboard and held it in front of him as he got out of the car.

"Hi, Aunt Gertrude," he greeted her. "We'd like to have you meet a friend of ours."

The tall, graying woman gave a shriek and almost lost her balance trying to get away from her nephew. Joe slowly but relentlessly pursued her.

"Get away from me, Joe Hardy!" Aunt Gertrude cried. "Get away, I say!"

Joe laughed. "Okay, Aunty," he said impishly. "But that's no way to win friends!" He started up the path toward the back door, and Frank joined him.

"Don't you dare take that horrible thing into the house!" Aunt Gertrude called after them. "If you must keep it, put it in your workshop where decent people won't have to look at it."

Later, after a quick shower and a change of clothes, the boys drove downtown and purchased a new tent. Then they hurried home and sat down with their mother and aunt to an appetizing dinner of roast beef and vegetables. Mrs. Hardy calmly accepted their announcement that they planned to go back to Skull Mountain that evening.

The talk soon turned to Fenton Hardy, who had been away from home for the past two weeks.

"What kind of case is he working on?" Frank asked.

"I don't know," Mrs. Hardy confessed. "Your father likes to keep the details of his work to himself." She smiled at the boys. "I suppose he feels I'll have less to worry about that way."

The boys had just finished eating when they heard a rattletrap car chug into the driveway. A moment later Chet Morton came into the dining room, greeted the Hardys cordially, then took an extra plate, knife, and fork from the sideboard. He drew a chair up to the table, spread a napkin carefully in his lap, and beamed at Aunt Gertrude.

Chet's visits often coincided with his friends' meal hours. The Mortons lived on a farm and always ate at least an hour earlier than the Hardys did.

"You're too late, Chet," Frank told him. "We've finished dinner."

Chet groaned. He looked at his watch. "Gosh," he said plaintively, "I came as quick as I could."

Joe could not help laughing at the woebegone expression on Chet's face. Next time, he promised, as Aunt Gertrude went into the kitchen, the Hardys would keep a filled plate for their pal.

Aunt Gertrude returned bearing a seven-layer chocolate nut cake. Chet's eyes lit up when he saw it.

"This is for the camp," Aunt Gertrude told her nephews.

Chet's face quivered slightly as he watched her pack the cake neatly in a box. "Camp? What camp?"

"Bob Carpenter's camp on Skull Mountain," Joe said. "Frank and I are working with him and Dick Ames on the reservoir mystery."

"I read about the water shortage," Chet said. "But what are you fellows doing up there?" He could not take his eyes off the cakebox.

Frank told him of their experiences, but he carefully omitted any reference to the skulls.

Joe, sensing Frank's plan, concealed a smile. "Why don't you come with us, Chet?" he said casually. "You can help eat the cake."

The stout boy beamed at the suggestion, then eyed Frank and Joe suspiciously. "I don't know," he said dubiously. "Every time I get mixed up with you two, something happens to make me regret it."

"Nonsense, Chet," Frank said. "What can happen to you on a camping trip?"

"Plenty of things—with you two around," Chet retorted.

"Well, if you don't want to go—" Frank said, shrugging. He looked at his brother. "Guess we'd better get started, Joe."

Joe nodded and picked up the cakebox. He

lifted the lid slightly open for another look and smacked his lips appreciatively.

This was more than Chet could bear. "Wait, fellows!" he begged. "I'll go with you!"

The three boys drove to the Morton farm. Chet ran into the house to pack some clothes. When he returned, the Hardy boys saw that he carried more food than camping paraphernalia.

"No telling how long we'll have to stay up there," Chet explained.

Evening shadows were falling by the time they climbed up the mountainside, then made the comparatively easy descent to the camp. Bob and Dick welcomed the three boys warmly.

"Glad to have you aboard," Bob said when Chet was introduced to him. Then they all sat down in Carpenter's Cottage to a snack of milk, sandwiches, and a slice of the cake. In a corner of the shack, Frank noticed a stack of white-painted shingles.

"Did you discover where the water is escaping?" he eagerly asked Bob.

The engineer's face clouded. "No," he said. "Dick and I rowed completely around the reservoir dropping shingles in the water. Then we watched to see if any of them drifted so as to reveal a current. We didn't find a thing. We gave up and brought the shingles back here."

"It beats me," Dick said. "All we know so far

is that the water rises during the day and sinks at night. The depth is never more than twenty-feet."

"Could there be a leak in the dam?" Joe asked.

Bob shook his head. "No," he said. "We've been over every inch of it." The tall engineer was silent for a moment. "There's only one possibility," he said.

He told them that when he was a student in college, he had made a careful study of the geology of the Bayport area. In his reading, he had come across a geologist's speculation that millions of years before, the Tarnack River had been blocked by a moraine, a huge mass of sand, rock, and other debris deposited by a glacier that had covered the entire region.

The geologist believed that the river had worn an outlet underground to the Atlantic Ocean. Later, upheavals had caused the Tarnack to change its course, eating a path through the moraine and settling into its present bed.

"If the theory is correct," Bob finished, "somewhere nearby there's a subterranean passage to the sea!"

Frank's eyes opened wide in amazement. "And you believe that the water from the reservoir is escaping through the ancient outlet?"

Bob nodded.

"Wow!" exclaimed Joe. "What a story!"

"But wouldn't the men who built the dam have discovered the tunnel when they diverted the river from the valley?" Frank persisted.

"If the tunnel started from the river bottom, yes," Bob admitted. "If there is such an outlet, it must be higher up—on one of the slopes."

"If we could only find it," Dick said, "our troubles would be over."

"*If!*" Bob laughed. "That's the trouble with theories! They're full of *ifs*!" He yawned. "I don't know about you fellows—but I'm going to get some shut-eye!"

The others agreed that it was time to turn in, and Frank and Joe went to help Chet pitch a pup tent next to theirs. Soon the boys were asleep.

Some time later a shriek from Chet split the night. "Help!" he yelled. "Take it away!"

CHAPTER IV

Sailor Hawkins

As FRANK and Joe ducked out of their tents, Bob and Dick burst from the shack.

Chet was kneeling at the opening to his tent, staring at something inside. He held a flashlight, but his hand shook so violently that Frank took it from him.

"Chet, what is it?" he asked anxiously.

Chet was frozen. He lifted his arm slowly and pointed. "There—on my pillow!" he whispered.

The boys' eyes followed their friend's outstretched arm. Staring at them from the cot was a human skull!

"I woke up when I felt something c-cold touching my cheek," Chet stammered, "and there it was—right against my face!" He shivered. "Ugh!"

Joe, shining his flashlight about the interior of the tent, suddenly asked, "Chet, what did you do with your clothes?"

"Clothes? Why, I put them right there—" Chet's jaw dropped as he looked at the canvas sack which had held his camping duds.

"Holy smoke!" he yelped. "They're gone!" Suddenly the boy stared at the soft earth beside the empty sack, and bent down for a closer look. "Hey!" he cried out. "Bring the light here!"

Frank shone the beam on the spot at which Chet pointed. The ground was marked with the print of a naked foot. One toe was missing!

"Joe, look!" Frank pointed excitedly. "The mountain man's tracks!"

Joe nodded grimly. "We've got a lot to settle with that guy! Maybe the landslide and the skulls, the explosion, and now Chet's clothes!"

"Do you think the mountain man could be responsible for the smoke, too?" Dick asked.

"Could be," Frank asserted. He looked out of the tent toward the shadowy mountain peak. "I'd give up a month of my vacation to know where he is right now!"

"I don't want to know," said Chet. "Every time I think of him sneaking here—" His glance rested on the skull. "What about that thing?"

"We thought you'd want to keep it," Frank said with a grin.

"It's all yours," Chet said firmly.

Frank chuckled and took the skull outside.

Bob grinned and said, "I'll put it in my duffel bag with the other two."

"A collection of skulls!" remarked Joe. "It's not so funny, when you figure they stand for danger."

Early the next day the brothers again set out to trail the mountain man. Joe had supplied Chet with shirt and pants which fitted like a sausage skin. Frank had contributed socks and a pair of boots, but these were so tight for the plump boy, he had decided to remain at camp.

The Hardys followed the footprints down and across the mountain through stretches of scrub and shale. Several times they lost the trail, but picked it up again on soft earth.

After a long, hot scramble they emerged from the trees and saw a cabin situated on the cleared slope above the reservoir. Nothing moved except a column of smoke which drifted lazily from an iron stack.

As they approached the cabin, Joe plucked at Frank's sleeve and pointed off to the left. Frank looked in that direction and nodded.

The footprints led unmistakably to several large fresh-cut tree stumps at the edge of the forest. Nearby were huge piles of neatly split firewood. Why, the boys wondered, had so much been cut? Certainly not just for the tiny cabin's fireplace or stove!

"I think we'll have a talk with the owner of this place," Frank decided.

They walked quietly down the hillside, then

stopped short. Inside the dilapidated house a hoarse voice was singing a rollicking sea chantey!

"Sailor Hawkins!" Joe said, grinning.

The boys winced as the voice went sour on a high note. They stepped onto the porch. Immediately, a parrot chained to a wooden stand screamed at them.

"Avast, ye lubbers!" The brightly plumed bird craned his neck, then set up a furious squawking. "Man the topsail, me hearties! Lend a hand there—or I'll keelhaul ye!"

Frank and Joe laughed loudly.

The parrot flapped his wings noisily. "Keelhaul ye! Keelhaul ye! Keelhaul ye!"

A short, squat man with a rolling gait ran out on the porch and lifted his hand threateningly at the parrot. "Pipe down, ye blighter. Or I'll give ye the back o' me hand!"

The bird subsided with several protesting squawks and the man turned to Frank and Joe. "Now then, mateys," he said, hitching his trousers with a nautical gesture, "who are ye?"

"I'm Frank Hardy," the older boy told the man. "This is my brother Joe. We were out walking. You're Sailor Hawkins, aren't you?"

"Captain Hawkins," the man corrected him with sudden dignity. "Least, I used to be—when I had me own square-rigger."

"Isn't this an odd place for a sailor to be?" Joe inquired.

"Aye, mate, it is that," Hawkins assured him. He looked around and shook his head gloomily. "I never would've come here if me ship hadn't cracked up on a reef." He sighed heavily. "Split every timber of her!"

"Can't you go back to sea?" Frank asked.

Sailor Hawkins sighed again. "Ah, laddie, I wish I could! But I'm too old for them new-fangled vessels!" He glared at the boys suddenly. "But I aint too old to fight for me rights!"

"What do you mean?" asked Joe.

Hawkins jerked his thumb. "This cabin—that's what I mean!" he shouted. "I built her meself! Put every board an' nail in her!" He stepped off the porch and scooped up a handful of dirt. "An' the land's mine, too! I been livin' alone here seven years, an' when ye been squattin' seven years—the land is your'n!"

He returned to the porch and stared at the boys suspiciously. "Mark me, mateys," he said, stubbing a blunt forefinger against Frank's chest for emphasis, "if any o' them smart-alecky engineers try to run water over me property, I'll blow 'em higher than a mainmast!" He grabbed up a rifle from the porch to show that he meant what he said.

The Hardys hastily assured Hawkins that they had no intention of destroying his property. He appeared somewhat mollified. But he was no more helpful than Potato Annie had been when they questioned him about the mystifying events on Skull Mountain.

Hawkins swore he had no idea what the smoke or explosions meant. He had never seen the shaggy-haired man of the mountain.

"We noticed someone has cut down a great deal of timber above you at the edge of the forest," Frank remarked.

Hawkins glared at him. "Aye," he said. "I did. A man can cut wood on his own property, can't he?"

"It's an awful lot of wood," Joe replied.

"Yes," Frank added, "and it could make a lot of smoke!"

The little man glared at the boys. "Sink me if I don't think ye working with them engineers!" he countered.

When the brothers admitted that this was true, Hawkins' face flushed. "Get off me land 'fore I blast ye off!" he roared, fingering his rifle.

As the boys stepped from the porch, the voice of the parrot screamed after them, "I'll keelhaul ye! Keelhaul ye! Keelhaul ye!"

Joe looked at Frank and grinned. "Pleasant customers! Maybe Hawkins is one of those night-time snipers."

"Could be. I don't think he's the fellow with the missing toe, though. His feet are too short and wide."

Frank and Joe walked up to the tree stumps

at the edge of the forest where they had last seen the footprints.

"We'll follow these tracks until we find who's at the end of them!" Frank declared.

But the trail ended a few hundred feet deeper in the woods. Whoever had left the footprints had vanished over a stretch of sheer rock.

Disappointed, the boys turned back. They had just reached the clearing above Hawkins' cabin when Joe suddenly whispered, "Hold it!" He pulled Frank back. "Look—on the porch!"

CHAPTER V

The Missing Scientist

TALKING earnestly with Hawkins on the porch was a tall, thin stranger.

"Wonder who he is?" queried Joe. He and Frank were crouched behind some shrubs at the edge of the woods.

Frank shook his head. The visitor looked around uneasily, then bent close to Hawkins and went on speaking.

Both boys listened intently, but the voices were too far away. Finally the stranger departed down the slope.

"I sure wish we could follow him," said Joe as the man's figure grew smaller and smaller.

"So do I," Frank agreed. "But with no trees for cover he'd be sure to spot us. Come on! Let's get back to the camp."

It was noon when the boys arrived at Carpenter's shack. From there they could see that Chet had joined Bob and Dick in the boat. The youth was standing precariously on one of the seats, probing with a long pole at a part of the slope which was under water.

"Any luck?" Frank called as he and Joe walked down to the shore.

"Not yet!" Bob yelled. "If there's an underground outlet in this valley, we haven't found it!"

"Take it easy, Chet," Joe called, grinning. "That pole's likely to throw you!"

As Chet twisted his head to make a retort, the pole caught in some brambles. The rowboat shot out from under his feet. For one agonizing instant, Chet dangled helplessly from the end of the pole. Then the shaft broke with a sharp crack, and the boy plopped into the water!

Chet rose to the surface, splashing and sputtering. On the shore Frank and Joe were doubled up with laughter. Bob and Dick could not help grinning.

Chet was indignant. "Don't—see—what's—so—funny!" he spluttered.

Dick rowed the boat close to the youth, and Bob reached over and hauled him in. As Dick pulled for the small floating dock, Chet sat dejected and dripping in the bottom of the boat. He surveyed himself dismally and lamented, "As if I wasn't hard up for clothes already, *this* had to happen!"

"Never mind, Chet," Frank reassured him as the rowboat docked, "I'll drive back to Bayport and bring you some more."

"You will?" Chet said, relieved, "Golly, that'll be swell!"

Frank turned to his brother. "I'll look in on Mother and Aunt Gertrude. You'd better stay here and keep an eye on things."

Bob looked at Frank. "What happened this morning?"

"Joe will tell you about it, Bob. The sooner I start, the quicker I'll get back. See you all later." He took a sandwich and apple for lunch, eating them on the trail which led to the parked convertible.

The woods was dim and quiet. Now and then a bird stirred among the branches. Suddenly there came a loud crash from a clump of heavy bushes beyond the path.

Frank stopped and listened. He wondered if he had startled a deer, and stood waiting for the animal to thrash off into the brush. But all was silent.

"That was no deer," Frank decided.

Stepping softly, he made his way to the clump of shrubs. Cautiously he parted it. Nothing there!

"Somebody was following me," Frank thought. "He probably fell down and then sneaked away so I wouldn't find him."

The shaft broke and Chet plopped into the water

He returned to the path and continued downward, keeping an ear open for his follower. But he heard nothing.

After a while the trail wound steeply down between tall trees and the light grew dimmer. Not a breath of air was moving. Frank rounded a bend and stopped short with a gasp!

Swinging lightly in mid-air was a human skull!

A moment later the startled boy saw the heavy black thread by which the grinning object was hanging from a branch.

"Whew!" Frank gave a little laugh. "You scared me, Smiley!"

Then he slipped into the woods to search for the person who had hung up the grisly surprise.

"He hasn't been gone long," Frank thought. "The skull is still moving." He found no one.

Frank returned to the path, took down the skull, and placed it next to a tree.

"Whoever did this trick is a slippery operator," he thought grimly, and wondered if it were the wild-looking mountain man.

An hour later, when Frank mounted the steps of the Hardy front porch, his father opened the door. "Dad!" Frank exclaimed. "Gosh, I'm glad to see you! When did you get back? Is your latest case solved?"

Fenton Hardy laughed and slapped his son on the back affectionately. "One question at a time," he said. "Where's Joe?"

As Frank started to explain, Mr. Hardy led the boy into his study and closed the door.

"Now," he said, "suppose you start at the beginning."

Frank did so, and Fenton Hardy listened attentively, laughing heartily when his son came to Chet's misadventure in the rowboat.

"That's the whole story, Dad," Frank concluded. He added gloomily, "So far, we haven't made much progress toward clearing up the case."

The famous detective smiled. "Solving mysteries is pretty much a problem of elimination, son. The more suspects and clues you can eliminate, the closer you are to the real criminals."

"That's just the trouble," said Frank. "We have too many suspects and clues." He looked thoughtful. "There's one thing I feel sure of, though. This is not just a matter of some poor squatters trying to hold onto their land. Keeping the reservoir empty is too big a trick for Potato Annie or Hawkins to pull off alone."

"I think you're right, Frank." Mr. Hardy leaned forward significantly. "The main thing is to find the motive for the crime. When you know that, you'll be well on your way to catching the criminal."

"Thanks, Dad," said Frank. "I'll remember that. What about your case? Can you tell me about it?"

Mr. Hardy explained that he was working on

an assignment for the Ace Laboratories in Pomford, Illinois.

A month before, Dr. Carl Foster, a scientist-engineer in charge of a project at the laboratories, had been granted a week's leave of absence. The scientist had not been seen since. The chief of the laboratories was frantic.

"I questioned all his employees, of course," Mr. Hardy went on. "I also went to the hotel where Dr. Foster had been living. I found these scraps in his wastebasket. It was made of wicker and these had got stuck in the woven bottom." He took two torn pieces of paper from his wallet and handed them to Frank.

"They're parts of a telegram," Frank observed. He studied them carefully. On one were the typed letters: LEN. On the other piece was the word BAY.

"Could BAY be part of Bayport?" the boy asked.

"It could," his father admitted. "It might also mean Bay Ridge, Bayview, Hudson Bay, and a thousand and one other cities, towns, villages, and waterways in North America."

There was a knock on the study door. It was Mrs. Hardy. "Why, Frank! You're home!" she exclaimed.

The youth explained that he had returned to obtain some clothes for Chet. "And I guess I'd better hurry out to the Morton farm," he went on. "Chet will be in a stew until he is wearing his own things!"

Mrs. Hardy smiled. "Say hello to the Mortons for me," she said. "And, Frank," she called after the retreating boy, "please stop at a plumber's shop and ask if he can come out here today and repair a leaking faucet!"

"Tell him it's an emergency!" Aunt Gertrude poked her head into the hall. "We can't afford to waste a drop of water in this town!"

Frank drove to a shop whose sign read "J. P. Kleng, Plumber." A tiny bell tinkled as he opened the door, and a surly-looking man with red hair came from the rear of the store.

He studied Frank unpleasantly as the boy told him of the leaking faucet. "What do you expect me to do about it?" he asked.

Frank stared at him in surprise. "Fix it!"

Kleng turned his back abruptly and started for the rear of the store.

Frank was annoyed. "Isn't it a plumber's job to help Bayport conserve water until the reservoir is ready?" he demanded.

At this, the man turned and shot Frank an odd look. "Why don't you try another plumbing shop? he suggested. "I work alone. Don't have much time to go out on calls."

"What does he do, then?" thought Frank. He had a feeling there was something behind the fellow's strange behavior. But he would have to find a plumber, and he wanted to return to Skull Mountain as quickly as possible.

"Could you recommend another plumber?" he asked the man.

"Sure." Kleng went to a desk littered with account books and papers, and took an office letterhead from one of the drawers. Hastily he scribbled the name of a nearby shop and thrust the paper toward Frank.

"Thanks," said Frank, folding the paper and placing it in his pocket.

Outside, the boy paused. "Something about Kleng rings false," he thought. Slowly he took out the folded paper the plumber had given him.

The fragments of two words seemed to leap out at him:

LEN

BAY

Frank's eyes widened. He unfolded the sheet. The top of the letterhead read: J. P. Kleng, Plumber. Centered below it was the word *Bayport*.

The boy rapidly refolded the paper to its original creases. The same letters again stood out.

Frank could not conceal his excitement. He was thinking of the two pieces of the telegram Fenton Hardy had found in Dr. Foster's hotel room? Could the names *Kleng* and *Bayport* have been in that telegram? It was a clue worth tracing!

As Frank was walking to his car, he noticed a tall, thin man stride past him. It was the fellow Frank and Joe had seen talking to Sailor Hawkins! Frank ducked into a nearby doorway.

The man went into Kleng's plumbing shop!

CHAPTER VI

Two Masked Men

WHEN the man had gone inside, Frank walked past the window of the shop. He was just in time to see Kleng and the stranger disappear into the rear of the store.

The youth debated whether to watch the shop and trail the tall stranger when he came out, or report the new developments to his father. He decided in favor of the latter. It seemed likely that Kleng was in some way involved with the disappearance of the scientist, and Fenton Hardy would want to know this as soon as possible. Frank jumped into the convertible and headed for home.

Mr. Hardy was excited when he heard his son's story. "If Kleng and the thin man are mixed up in Dr. Foster's disappearance," he pointed out, "they'll meet again." The investigator said he would like to know when, but the operatives who usually worked for him were on other assignments.

"I have an idea," said Frank. "Maybe I can help you." He made a telephone call, but the line was busy. It was an hour later that he reached his friend Callie Shaw to ask if she and Chet's sister Iola would help to scout Kleng's shop.

"I'll be glad to, Frank," she said. "But what should we look for?"

Frank explained his suspicions of the plumber. "I thought maybe you and Iola could round up some of the girls and take turns going in the store on errands or window shopping nearby. Keep the place covered. If you see a tall, thin man go in, call my father at once."

Callie chuckled. "It sounds exciting. I'll round up my female detectives right away!"

"Be careful, Callie. Don't let Kleng catch on!"

"I'll do the best I can!" the girl promised.

Frank left for the camp, stopping to pick up Chet's clothes on the way. Mrs. Morton insisted that he stay for dinner. Afterward, Chet's father showed Frank some new milking machines. When Frank was finally able to excuse himself, it was growing dark.

He headed the convertible toward Skull Mountain. After about fifteen minutes, he slowed down and turned off the concrete highway onto the dirt road which led to the mountain. He had gone only a short distance when, in the mirror, he saw the glare of a single headlight bearing down on him.

Frank realized it was the headlight of a motorcycle. The boy slowed down, glancing at the speedometer. "I don't get it!" he muttered. "A trooper doesn't hand you a ticket for driving twenty on a country road!"

The motorcycle drew abreast of the convertible. Frank gasped. There were two riders. They were not troopers! Both wore masks!

"Pull over!" the driver ordered, and crowded the convertible to the side of the road. Frank turned off the ignition.

The motorcycle halted alongside and the men got off. One was short with a thick, muscular body. Frank's heart quickened. The other, who had been driving, was tall and thin!

"Get out!" the thin man ordered.

Warily Frank obeyed. He tried to distinguish the features of the two men, but their hatbrims were pulled low and their masks concealed their eyes, noses, and mouths.

"What's the idea?" Frank asked.

"You're Fenton Hardy's kid," the thin man stated. "What's your father doing about the old man's disappearance?" Frank looked at the speaker quizzically.

"You know who we mean!" the thin man snapped. "What's Hardy found out about him?"

"I don't know what you're talking about!" Frank declared.

The thin man shrugged. "There are ways to make you talk," he said, turning to his companion. "Shall we give the kid a demonstration?"

"Sure, Sweeper."

Frank desperately scanned the dirt road for an approaching car. But no light glimmered in the darkness.

"Another thing," Sweeper went on, "stop nosing into other people's business on the mountain. There are plenty of graves up there—but there's room for more."

"Forget the talk," the shorter man said roughly. "Let me work on him."

As the man stepped toward him, Frank desperately decided to try an old trick. Suddenly he pretended to see someone behind the men. "Joe!" he yelled. "Over here!"

Caught off guard, the two thugs half turned. Instantly Frank darted into the darkness, then dove behind a clump of bushes.

Then he heard the men's voices and realized they were searching the car!

Footsteps approached, and Frank shrank back against the grass, feigning unconsciousness. Through almost closed eyes, he saw the two men staring down at him.

The thin man kicked him hard in the ribs. Frank stifled a grunt and did not move.

"He's out like a light," Sweeper exclaimed in disgust. "Must have hit his head. Come on! We can't get any information out of him."

Frank waited until he heard the roar of their vehicle. It backfired, then disappeared into the night with its motor throbbing in a peculiar, uneven rhythm.

Frank stood up shakily and returned to the convertible. The glove compartment was open and the front seat was littered with keys, flashlight bulbs, and crumpled papers and maps. Dazed, Frank drove slowly back to the highway to a farmhouse and asked permission to use the telephone.

The farmer directed him to the telephone and he placed a call to his father. "What's wrong, son?" Fenton Hardy queried when he heard Frank's unsteady voice. "You sound as if you're sick!"

"Not sick, Dad. Just a little shaky. Don't worry."

Frank told his father of the incident. Mr. Hardy was greatly interested in the possibility that one of the men was the tall, thin stranger Frank had seen on the mountain and later entering Kleng's shop.

"It looks to me," the boy continued, "as if the mystery of the disappearing water is somehow tied up to your missing scientist!"

"It certainly does, Frank," the detective agreed. "And these fellows are dangerous."

After promising his father to be careful, Frank hung up and thanked the farmer for the use of his telephone.

It was late when Frank arrived at the camp. Joe and Chet greeted him with enthusiasm, which changed to concern when Frank told them all that had happened.

"Zowie!" Chet exclaimed, shaking his head. "I'm not the only one who's had troubles!"

Frank grinned, and gave his friend the package of clothes. "Here, Chet," he said. "Now you can join us when we go after the masked men!"

"Not me!" Chet declared, cradling the package in his arms and walking toward his tent. "I'm too delicate for strong-arm stuff!"

Frank noticed that the two engineers were not in camp. "Where are Bob and Dick?" he asked his brother.

"They went down to the reservoir," Joe replied. "This afternoon Bob painted a white stripe on a slab of rock, to mark the water line. They've gone to see how fast the level is falling."

As the boys walked toward their tents, Joe brought Frank up to date on his activities. That afternoon he had seen another column of smoke rising from the crest of the mountain. Joe had sighted the spot carefully, but when he had

climbed the mountain, he had found no trace of a
fire.

"Same old story," he concluded gloomily. "I
found nothing!"

Chet poked his head out of his pup tent.
"Hey!" he called. "How about some chow? I'm
starved!"

The boys went into the shack. Chet whistled
noisily while he made hot chocolate. With the
rich drink they had sandwiches, and what remained of Aunt Gertrude's cake.

"I'm convinced that more important people
than the squatters are interested in keeping Tarnack Reservoir from filling," Frank declared as
they ate. "I think we've got to look for something
that ties in with Dr. Foster, the scientist Dad is
searching for."

"I don't see the connection," Joe remarked as
he watched Chet devour another sandwich.

"I don't either, Joe. Not yet," said his brother.
"But everything I found out today points to a tie-
up between Kleng, Dr. Foster, and the thin man
called Sweeper. And we saw that thin man on
the mountain!"

"It's true." Joe nodded. "By the way, Bob's
still convinced the water is running out through
an underground channel."

"I don't believe there is any old tunnel," Chet
grumbled.

"How else can the water escape?" Frank asked.
They thought in silence for a moment.

"What I'd like to know is," Joe said, "why does
the channel drain off the water at night only?"

"You've got me there," Frank admitted. "But
first we must prove that the underground channel
exists and one way to do that is by planting floats
in the reservoir and leaving them in at night!"

"And if the tunnel exists, we can watch for the
stuff at the other end!" Joe said excitedly.

"But where is the other end?" Chet asked skep-
tically.

"According to the book Bob read, the underground river empties into the bay at Bayport,"
Frank replied.

The boys were silent for a moment, each considering the possibilities of the plan.

"Hey!" Chet said suddenly. "I smell smoke!"

The boys sniffed. "See if something's burning
on the stove," Frank suggested.

Chet rose heavily from his chair and went to
the stove. "Nothing here," he reported. Then he
stared. Wisps of smoke were curling through the
floor boards of the wooden shack!

"Fire!" he yelled, pointing to the floor.

Frank and Joe leaped to their feet. "Come on,
everybody out!" yelled Joe.

"Take that bucket of water with you!" Frank
ordered, pointing behind his brother.

Joe grabbed up the bucket as Frank ran for the door. He pulled on the knob, but the door refused to open. Frank yanked again with all his strength.

"Chet!" he gasped. "Give me a hand!" The heavy-set boy also gripped the doorknob, and together they strained at it.

"It must be jammed," Frank breathed. "It won't budge!"

"Try the windows!" Joe shouted.

They ran to the two windows in the shack, then drew back. Flames were already licking the window sills!

Joe emptied the water bucket on them, but the blaze continued to mount.

"It's no use!" cried Chet. "We're trapped!"

CHAPTER VII

A Hatchet Job

DESPERATELY the boys looked for a means of escape. Lifting a chair, Frank hammered at the wooden door. It would not yield. Smoke billowed thickly through the cracks in the floor, and a tongue of flame licked greedily at a plank.

The smoke made the boys' eyes water. They began to cough. Then, just when it seemed there was no way out, they heard excited voices. A moment later the blade of an ax bit through the door!

"Bob—Dick!" Joe shouted. "Hurry!"

"Boy, will I be glad to see them!" Chet spluttered weakly.

"Grab anything you can carry!" Frank gasped.

Quickly the boys gathered armloads of papers, camping equipment, and engineering instruments. Chet scooped up clothing.

Blows from Bob's ax had split the wood at the

jamb. An instant later the door was flung back, and the boys ran into the open. They dropped their bundles and breathed deeply, filling their lungs with fresh mountain air.

Meanwhile, shouts of "Fire!" came from the reservoir and the boys could see some of the sounding crew running up the slope with buckets of water.

Bob and Dick were frantically shoveling sand from the nearby pile onto the flames. The Hardys and Chet pitched in, using whatever pots and pans they could lay hands on.

When the last flame was out, the boys and men stood gasping for breath.

"Frank," said Bob wearily, "what happened?"

"That's what we'd like to know!" Joe declared.

"A fire started under the shack," Frank went on, "and when we tried to run out, we couldn't get the door open."

"It was padlocked!" Dick said grimly.

"Padlocked!" Joe gasped.

"Yes," Bob replied. "Someone snapped the lock shut while you were inside!"

"And then set the fire!" Frank exclaimed.

"Golly," said Chet. "Who would do a thing like that?"

"Someone who is desperate to get rid of us," Dick replied bitterly.

The sounding crew watched silently as the Hardys searched carefully around the smoking shack for a clue to the arsonist. They found none.

Talking uneasily, the men started down the slope again. One of them said, "This party's getting too rough for me."

"That's all we need—" Bob remarked bitterly, "is for the crew to quit."

The boys and engineers examined the blackened shack and were relieved to see that the main damage was to the floor, windows, and door.

"We can fix it," Dick said. "We've got tools and lumber."

The Hardys helped Bob and Dick salvage whatever articles they could from the shack. Nearby, the engineers pitched two tents which Joe had rescued from the fire.

Bob told the boys that he had gained some specific information from the white stripe with which he had previously marked the high-water level of the reservoir that afternoon.

"When we got there tonight, the level of the water was one foot under the mark," he said. "But the rock itself was damp for four feet above the stripe!"

Dick summarized their findings. "During the afternoon the water rose four feet. And later five feet of it drained away!"

"We've checked it daily and find that the story is always the same."

"Sounds as if the flow is controlled in some way," said Joe.

Frank wanted to tell the engineers about his idea of planting articles in the reservoir at night, but he did not wish to arouse their hopes too soon. He caught Joe's eye, and the younger Hardy understood that he was not to mention the plan.

Early the next day, while the engineers repaired the shack, Frank and Joe went down to the reservoir and walked along the shore a few feet from the water. Chet trudged behind them.

The slope at the water's edge was dotted with rocks, patches of shrubs, and creeping vines which extended under the water. Did one of the tangled masses conceal the mouth of the tunnel?

The boys prodded the brush with long sticks, tearing away the thickly matted branches and leaves. The job was slow, difficult, and unrewarding.

Now and then they looked up and saw men with earphones and sounding equipment working around the shore.

When the sun was high overhead, one of the men gave a shrill whistle. He signaled the others and the crew climbed the hill, carrying their lunch boxes and gear into the shade of the trees above.

"They're going to have lunch, I bet," said Chet. "How about us?"

"Soon," Frank said briefly. Both Hardys were intent on their job.

After a while, Chet wiped his forehead. "Wow, is it hot!" The youth sat down heavily, then jumped up as if he had been shot. "Ow!" he yelled.

He put his hand to the seat of his pants and gingerly pulled out a huge thorn. "That's what I get for letting you two talk me into hunting for an old tunnel!" he said disgustedly.

Joe turned to his brother. "What can you do with a guy like that?" he asked.

Frank looked speculatively at the water. "We might duck him," he suggested.

"We might at that!" Joe's eyes lighted up at the idea.

Chet blanched. "Don't you dare!" he pleaded.

"Come on, Joe! Grab him!" yelled Frank.

Laughingly the Hardys took hold of their friend. Frank clutched Chet's struggling arms and shoulders while Joe held his feet.

The stout boy shouted helplessly, "Oh, come on, fellows, let me down!"

They started to swing the spluttering youth toward the water.

"One!" Frank counted. "Two—"

Suddenly a metallic sound rang out from the woods above them.

"Hold it! Listen!" exclaimed Frank.

Again and again the noise echoed from the mountainside over the silent sun-baked valley.

"Come on!" Frank raced up the slope with Joe at his side and Chet slipping and sliding along behind.

Panting, they reached the woods as the sound stopped. A moment later there was thrashing in the underbrush.

Joe bounded up the slope after the invisible figure, but in a few minutes the crackling of brush ceased. He searched among the trees and beat the bushes, but could find no one. Disappointed, he started down the hill.

"Over here, Joe," called Frank.

The younger boy hastened to his brother and Chet who stood under a large tree near the edge of the woods. Without a word, Frank pointed to the ground.

Six sets of electronic sounding equipment lay smashed beyond repair.

As Joe groaned and shook his head, the men of the sounding crew came running down the hill.

"I knew it!" exclaimed a tall man. "As soon as I heard the noise!"

"Another hatchet job!" said one of his companions. "We should never have left the gear here, but we decided to take a hike and the stuff was too heavy to carry."

Bitterly the crew gathered up the broken pieces and started back to the shack to report to Bob Carpenter.

"Those men were being watched," Frank said quietly. "Probably we are too."

"Oh, that's great!" croaked Chet. "Why did I ever leave home?"

The three started walking toward Bob's shack. Suddenly Frank exclaimed, "Look!" He pointed to the crest of the mountain. *A thin column of smoke was rising from it!*

"Come on!" he exclaimed. "We're going to find that fire!"

"Wait!" wailed Chet. "What about lunch?" But the Hardys were already climbing up the slope. Chet groaned and followed.

Soon they found themselves skirting Potato Annie's garden. The old woman had been pulling turnips, carrots, and beets. As the boys hastened past, she picked up a basket laden with the vegetables, then hobbled up into the woods.

"Wonder where she's taking all that food," Joe said.

"Don't know," replied Frank, "and we can't stop now to find out. Maybe she sells 'em."

"We'd better check on her later," said Joe. He glanced back. Chet was puffing to catch up, but the woman was hurrying away fast.

Climbing steadily, the three youths hoped to reach the smoke before it vanished. As they crossed a small clearing, a shot rang out.

"What was that?" Chet yelped, ducking.

They looked behind them to see Sailor Hawkins standing among the trees, his rifle still smoking. He shook his fist at them. "Get off the mountain!" he roared. "Ye no-good swabs!" The boys hurried into the woods.

"Who's he?" Chet demanded, glancing behind him in time to see Hawkins disappear down the slope.

"Just a friend," Joe replied airily.

"Some friends you've got!" Chet retorted. "When they're not throwing rocks at you, they're throwing bullets!"

Frank and Joe laughed. Then they looked up toward the smoke. It was gone!

"Oh, no, not again!" exclaimed Joe.

Frank considered. "We've come this far, so we may as well keep going," he decided.

They had just resumed their climb when they heard the sound of an ax striking wood. It seemed to be only a few hundred yards away!

The boys looked at one another excitedly. "Maybe that's our hatchet man!" Frank said softly. "Let's go!"

Half running, the three made their way through the woods toward the sound. Except for the echoing blows of the ax, the forest was strangely still.

They clambered over scattered rocks and skirted a cliff. As the ax rang more loudly, they crept forward.

Suddenly the noise stopped. The boys halted and stared ahead anxiously. Had someone spotted them?

They waited a moment for the chopping to resume. When it did not, Frank broke into a run, motioning the others to follow. Soon they came to a small clearing.

Frank pointed to the stumps of several fresh-cut trees. He went over to them and examined the surrounding earth. "Look here," he said.

Joe's eyes followed his finger. Pressed into the soft earth were the footprints of the man with the missing toe!

Frank traced the prints for a short distance and saw that they followed a narrow dirt path. He beckoned to the other two.

Walking stealthily, wondering how close they might be to their quarry, the boys trailed the mysterious prints. Once they lost them, but Joe found a fresh-cut tree limb the man apparently had dropped, and they soon picked up the trail.

As they hurried forward, Chet's eyes fell on a pocketknife lying beside a tree. He stared at it disbelievingly. Engraved on it were the initials C.M. "Hey!" he called softly. "Look what I found!"

Frank and Joe joined their friend. "It's my knife! I had it in the pocket of the pants that were stolen!"

"Swell, Chet!" Joe congratulated him. "If we

catch up with this guy, maybe you'll get back your clothes!"

Buoyed up by their find, the searchers hurried forward. Suddenly the trail vanished in an open patch of grass.

As the boys paused, they heard a faint sound in the woods to their right. Frank signaled the others to follow him. They crept forward, taking care not to step on twigs.

A moment later they stopped abruptly at the edge of a small clearing. On a fallen bough sat a gaunt-faced man so thin that his bones seemed to protrude from his flesh.

Frank nudged his brother and pointed to the fellow's right foot. It had only four toes!

Gray, shaggy hair hung down to the man's neck, and a matted beard covered his chest. He was eating a turnip, gulping it down without chewing, and on the ground beside him lay a dozen pieces of split wood and an ax.

His shirt was tattered and sleeveless. But he wore a new pair of khaki shorts. They hung on him in loose folds.

"My shorts!" exclaimed Chet.

The man stood up swiftly, dropping the half-eaten turnip. He fixed the boys with a fierce stare. Then he grabbed the ax and swung it around his head.

"Watch out!" Joe yelled. "He's going to throw it!"

CHAPTER VIII

A Disappearance

INSTANTLY the man lowered the ax. With a wild laugh, he fled into the woods.

"After him!" shouted Joe.

The boys chased the tall, bony creature through the woods at breakneck speed.

Suddenly he scooted into a deep gully. The boys crashed down the brush-covered slope behind him, but could see him nowhere. They searched amid the thick bushes and boulders.

"No use," said Joe, disgusted. "He's done it again."

"He must know this mountain like the back of his hand," Frank said with a sigh.

"Well, at least we know he's the man with the missing toe," Joe remarked as the boys climbed out of the ravine.

"And we know he stole my clothes!" Chet added heatedly.

"It's too bad he couldn't steal a tailor with them," Frank put in, grinning. "One pair of your shorts is big enough to make two or three outfits for him!"

Chet looked disgusted. "My best pair of shorts!"

Their conversation turned once more to the wild man. He had indeed set off the explosion near the boys' tents. The firewood he cut was probably the source of the smoke they had seen. But where had he come from? Why was he sabotaging the reservoir project?

"He must live on the mountain," Frank said. "I'll bet he's a hermit."

"I'd hate to meet that skull-toting guy in these woods on a dark night!" Chet declared. "Now let's get back to camp, fellows, please. I'm hungry!"

The boys descended to the shack and ate a late lunch. They found a note from Bob explaining that he and Dick had gone to Bayport to order more sounding equipment and would not be back until the next day.

"Tonight we'll drop some articles in the reservoir," said Frank, "and see if we can find them in the bay."

"How about shingles?" asked Joe, nodding to the pile in the corner.

"Nope. We need something easier to see. Too

bad we haven't some dye. That's often used for tracing currents."

The boys searched the shack and found an old decoy duck in the back of a cupboard. Joe guessed that the dam-builders had used it for hunting the autumn before. "There are some lakes near here," he said.

Chet found a large slab of yellow pine and an old barrel stave behind the shack.

Using paint from Bob's supply shelf, the boys made the duck white with red initials: F and J. They colored the pine slab red, and put red and white stripes on the barrel stave, which had a split in it. Then the articles were placed in the afternoon sun to dry.

At nightfall the boys gathered them up.

"Look, Chet, you don't have to come," said Frank. "There's no sense in all of us taking the risk."

"No sir," said Chet firmly, "I'm going with you."

"Good old Chet, you always come through in the pinch," said Joe.

Chet looked pleased, then said, "To tell you the truth, I'm not keen to stay up here alone with that creepy hermit running around."

"I don't blame you," Joe said with a chuckle as they made their way quietly down the slope to the reservoir.

The boys' scalps prickled as they stepped into Bob's rowboat and pushed off. *Were any unseen snipers watching them?* Tense and silent, they waited for the crack of a rifle.

Chet glanced around apprehensively as Frank rowed over the murky water. The squeak of the oars and the trickle of water from the blades were the only sounds.

"Let her ride," Joe said as the boat swung close to the opposite shore.

Frank hauled in the oars, and Joe put the duck in the water. Frank rowed on, keeping the craft a few feet from the shore. Then Joe and Chet quietly placed the pine slab and barrel stave overboard.

Quickly Frank headed for the dock where he hooked the boat to its mooring line. The boys stepped ashore and hurried up the hill to the shack. Not until they were inside did they speak.

"Whew! We made it!" Frank grinned in relief as Chet sank into a chair.

"It must have been the snipers' night off," said Joe.

"If that underground channel exists," said Frank, "at least one of those things ought to be sucked into it!"

"How long do you suppose it will take for this stuff to go through the tunnel?" Joe asked.

Frank thought a moment. "I don't know. If this channel were a straight flume or chute, the articles might pass through in a couple of hours. But the tunnel might not go the most direct way and there may be obstructions. It could take a couple of days."

"Besides," said Chet, "the water only flows at night."

"All the same," Joe put in, "we had better search for the stuff as soon as we can. It might go through more quickly than we think. Then the tide could carry it out of the bay, and we'd never know."

Frank said, "I'd like to drive back to Bayport tonight to check with Dad and Callie. How about you two?"

"Suits me," Joe replied.

"Me too," Chet said, glancing at his watch. "Do you think Aunt Gertrude will feel like a midnight snack?"

Joe grinned. "She will if you ask her!"

They packed a few things and Frank left a note telling Bob and Dick of the day's events and saying the boys would return in a day or two.

Aunt Gertrude was in bed reading when the three arrived at the Hardy home. When she heard that Chet had set his heart on having a slice of her pie or cake before going home, she good-naturedly put on a robe and came downstairs. Soon the boys were enjoying sandwiches, milk, and generous slices of cherry pie.

"Where's Dad?" Joe asked.

"He had a telephone call this evening and went out," Aunt Gertrude said. "He said he wouldn't be back until tomorrow. That's all he told me," she added with a sniff.

Chet ate the last crumb of his pie and announced that he must start for home. "I'll see you tomorrow," he told the boys. He beamed at Aunt Gertrude. "Thanks for the pie!"

The next day the boys were at breakfast when the telephone rang. Mrs. Hardy answered the call. "It's Callie," she told Frank. "She says she must see you right away!"

"Where is she?" Frank asked, pushing back his chair.

"In the drugstore—a few doors from Kleng's plumbing shop," his mother said.

"I'd better get right over!" Frank said excitedly, thrusting his arms into the sleeves of his jacket.

"I'll go with you!" Joe put in promptly.

"Okay, but hurry!" Frank called, rushing out the door. "I'll get the car."

Ten minutes later Frank parked in front of the drugstore. It was a bright, windy day and Callie's blond hair was blowing as she hurried to meet the boys.

"What happened?" Frank asked worriedly. "You look frightened!"

"I am," Callie said. "At least, I was," she amended with a little laugh. She looked nervously up and down the street, then beckoned the two boys into the doorway of a vacant store where they could not be seen so easily.

"None of us girls had any luck yesterday," she said, "so I went to Mr. Kleng's shop this morning. And while I was in there buying washers, the wind blew the screen door open and all the papers flew off Mr. Kleng's desk. Of course I helped him pick them up. And, Frank, one of them was a telegram! Well, when Mr. Kleng saw it in my hand, he was furious. I never saw a man so angry!" She shivered. "He snatched it away from me."

"Did you see what it said?" Joe asked.

"Yes, I couldn't help it. I think I remember all the words."

"Go ahead," said Frank, taking a notebook and pencil from his pocket.

"The message said: 'Syndicate convinced you are stalling. What's wrong? Can Retsof deliver? When?' And it was signed 'Ben.' "

"Retsof," Frank mused. "Sounds like a foreign name."

"Maybe it's in code," Joe suggested.

"Could be," Frank agreed, studying the name thoughtfully. "Yes!" he cried out. "It's Foster spelled backward!"

Joe was elated. "That's proof Kleng is mixed up in Dr. Foster's disappearance!"

The boys grinned at one another, and Frank

looked at Callie with admiration. "Do you know where the message came from?" he asked her.

"Chicago," Callie answered promptly. "And I have something else to tell you," she added, her eyes sparkling. "Guess who came to see Mr. Kleng while I was in there?"

"The tall, thin man!" Frank exclaimed.

"Yes," Callie said triumphantly. "Mr. Kleng called him 'Sweeper.'"

"I thought so," Frank remarked grimly. "Sweeper is the man we saw on the mountain, talking to Sailor Hawkins and one of the men who held me up."

Joe spoke up. "And Kleng might have been the other one. We'd better have a talk with him."

"You can't!" Callie exclaimed. "He locked up his shop right after I left. He said he was leaving town!"

The boys exchanged glances of dismay. If Kleng left Bayport, they might never solve the two mysteries.

"Did I do a good job for you?" Callie asked.

"You were a doll," Frank said warmly. "Come on. We'll drive you home."

At Callie's house Frank asked to see a telephone directory. "I'm going to look up Kleng's home address," he explained to Joe. "If he told Callie the truth, maybe he's still home packing."

Frank wrote down the street and number, then drove to the plumber's house.

It was a drab, two-story frame dwelling, set

back from the street by a short lawn. As the boys went up the steps to the porch, they saw that the shades were drawn.

No one answered the doorbell. Joe tried to peer through a window, but the shade completely shut off his view.

They returned to the car. As Joe got in, he looked over his shoulder. Was it his imagination —or had he glimpsed a woman's face staring at them from an upstairs window?

He told Frank about his suspicion, and his brother deliberated. "If it was Kleng's wife, he can't have gone away for good. We'll go back some other time and try our luck."

Mr. Hardy had returned when the boys arrived home. They showed him Frank's copy of the telegram Kleng had received, and he studied it with great care.

"We must do our best to keep track of Kleng," the detective remarked.

Frank told him of the possibility that the plumber had left Bayport. Mr. Hardy frowned.

"He may have gone to Chicago." He reached for the phone and dialed information in that city. While the call went through, he reread the telegram message. "I'll try to trace the sender of this message," he told the boys. "Through him we may pick up Kleng."

Frank and Joe left their father to complete his call.

As Frank closed the door to Mr. Hardy's study,

he said to Joe, "The sooner we take the *Sleuth* and begin looking for the articles we dropped into the reservoir last evening, the better. The tide will be going out in another hour."

The boys drove to the boathouse where they kept their trim white craft. Frank stepped into the cockpit and pushed the starter button.

The motor failed to catch. As Frank put out his hand to try again, the boys heard the uneven roar of a motorcycle behind the boathouse. Then it stopped.

Joe saw a tense look come over his brother's face. "That motorcycle!" Frank whispered. "It sounds like the one Sweeper was riding the night he held me up!"

CHAPTER IX

Tiger Trouble

FRANK leaped from the *Sleuth* and ran toward the rear of the boathouse. Joe followed, close on his brother's heels.

The motorcycle was parked in a nearby shed, but its rider was nowhere to be seen. In a corner of the flimsy building was a door leading to a boat landing.

"He must have gone that way!" Frank said.

He flung open the door and they rushed out onto the landing. A few feet away a tall, thin man wearing a tan jacket stood at the wheel of a speedboat.

"It's Sweeper!" Frank exclaimed softly.

The boys heard the sputtering roar of a motor, and the craft curved out into the bay. "Come on!" Frank cried, racing for the *Sleuth*. "We'll follow him!"

"Go ahead," Joe yelled. "I'll try to trace the owner of the motorcycle!"

Frank shouted, "Okay!" A moment later the *Sleuth* sped away from the boathouse and roared in pursuit of the other craft.

Joe went back to the shed and examined the motorcycle carefully. There was a leather pouch attached to the seat, but it contained only a pair of goggles and a few greasy rags.

Then he noticed that the vehicle bore the familiar red-and-black license plate issued by an adjoining state.

"Well, that's something to go on!" Joe told himself. He memorized the number. "This is a clue Dad can help me track down," he thought.

Joe returned to the convertible and headed for home. He was pleased to find his father there, and told him of the new developments.

Fenton Hardy telephoned the Motor Vehicle Bureau that had issued the motorcycle license plate. When he hung up, the detective told his son, "Looks as if you'd better check on a Timothy Kimball of Brookside."

"Brookside!" Joe exclaimed. "That's just across the state line! I could drive there in an hour. Kimball might be the man in the speed-boat—the one called Sweeper," he added.

"Don't make too many rapid deductions, son,"

his father cautioned. "Remember, the motorcycle may have been borrowed by a friend of Kimball —or it might even have been stolen."

Joe had to admit his father was right. "But I have no other lead to go on," he pointed out.

"Follow it up, certainly," said the detective, "but I think it would be wise to find out all you can about Kimball before you see him. The facts will help you size him up."

Mr. Hardy thought a moment, then went on, "Barney Matson, the city editor of the *Brookside News,* is an old friend of mine. If anyone can give you information, he can. Here, I'll write a little note to Barney." The detective scribbled something on a piece of paper. "Give him my regards."

"Thanks, Dad," Joe said gratefully.

Traffic was light, and Joe entered the office of the Brookside daily newspaper less than an hour later. The city editor sat alone at a long table. He beamed when Joe presented Fenton Hardy's note and explained his mission.

"Your dad was right. I can tell you some things about both Kimballs—father and son," Mr. Matson said, inviting Joe to be seated next to him.

The city editor said that the elder Kimball was president of a local construction firm. "He has a fairly solid reputation—personally and in his

business. But his son—" The editor broke off and
shook his head.

"What's the son's name?" Joe asked.

"Timothy Kimball Jr. He's a handsome fellow,
must be about thirty-one now. He's a bad apple,
although old Kimball seldom admits that."

The city editor went on to say that the son
had been irresponsible in his school days, and
had been accused of vandalism.

"The father always used his influence to get
the boy out of jams. Later, young Kimball took
up with some shady characters. The police have
suspected him of several jobs in the last few years.
But they never can pin anything on him."

Mr. Matson was interrupted by a man from the
copy desk and said he would have to get back to
work. Joe thanked the editor for his help, and
asked for the address of the Kimball Company.
As he was leaving, Mr. Matson said, "Watch your
step, Joe. Old Kimball's a tiger when he's mad!"

It was a short drive to the construction firm.
When Joe was admitted to the handsomely fur-
nished office of the president, the gray-haired,
ruddy-cheeked man rose from his chair, walked
around his large desk, and extended his hand to
the youth.

"My receptionist tells me you're Joe Hardy,"
Mr. Kimball said. "Aren't you Fenton Hardy's
son?"

"Yes, I am."

The man's manner was friendly, but Joe thought he looked uneasy as he asked, "Fenton Hardy, the detective?"

Joe nodded. Mr. Kimball motioned him to take a seat, and again sat down behind his imposing desk. "What brings you to see me, young man?" he asked after a moment. His hands began to fidget with a letter opener.

"Mr. Kimball, I found a motorcycle in Bayport registered in your name. I have a hunch it was stolen." Joe thought it best to reveal his suspicions little by little, taking his cues from the company president's reactions.

Mr. Kimball looked straight at Joe as he spoke. "I own a motorcycle," he admitted. "It's used by the company to carry messages from this office to field engineers. Now what makes you think it's been stolen?"

"I don't know for sure that it's been stolen. But the man I saw riding the motorcycle was familiar to me," Joe replied. "I had seen him before in rather suspicious circumstances."

Mr. Kimball stared at his hands, which still fumbled with the letter opener. "What does he look like?" he asked softly.

"A dark-haired young man, tall and thin," Joe told him. "He was wearing a tan jacket."

The paper knife fell from the man's fingers and his mouth twitched. "I'll see if there's a messenger in our employ who answers that description," he said, picking up the telephone.

When Mr. Kimball began to speak, he turned away from Joe and shielded his lips with his hand. The young detective strained to hear what the company president was saying, but he could understand only a few words. As Mr. Kimball put down the telephone, Joe noted that he was gripping it so tightly his knuckles were white. But when the man swung around, his face was bland.

"He's trying to cover up," Joe thought.

"There is such a man working for us," Mr. Kimball said pleasantly. "But you're mistaken about the motorcycle being stolen. The young man was sent to Bayport on an errand by my plant foreman."

Mr. Kimball gave a little laugh. "You must have confused him with someone else. My foreman tells me he has a fine record."

"I see," said Joe. Then he asked, "Would you mind telling me the man's name?"

Mr. Kimball shook his head firmly. "I don't think that would be proper." He glanced at a small clock on his desk, then rose. "And now, if you'll excuse me, I have an appointment."

Joe stood up also. He turned as if to leave, then asked suddenly, "Mr. Kimball, may I see a picture of your son?"

The gray-haired man stared at him. "What for?" he asked angrily.

"I have reason to believe he is the man I saw on the motorcycle," Joe told him quietly.

Mr. Kimball's face reddened and he took a step toward the boy. "Get out of here!" he ordered, his voice shaking. "I had an idea your father sent you to question me. Now I'm sure of it! What my son does is nobody's business but his and mine!" He raised his fist threateningly. "Get out!"

Joe returned to the car. He was sorry for Mr. Kimball, and sympathized with the man's loyalty to his son.

"But all the same," Joe said to himself, "I'll bet Timothy Kimball Jr. is the thug called Sweeper!"

Back in Bayport, Joe was surprised to find that Frank had not returned home. Mr. Hardy, too, was away on an investigation.

"This house is worse than a railroad station!" Aunt Gertrude complained. "People racing in and out any time they please, expecting Laura and me to run a twenty-four-hour restaurant service!"

Joe hugged his aunt affectionately. "Nobody minds making a stopover at this station as long as you're honoring the meal tickets!"

"A stopover!" Aunt Gertrude sniffed. "Your friend Chet Morton seems to think our dining-room table is the end of the line. We have to plan my grocery lists around that boy's appetite!"

"Chet!" exclaimed Joe. He was suddenly reminded of the articles they had planted in the reservoir. It would soon be time to set up a watch in the bay to determine whether the objects had been carried there by an underground stream. Chet could help him carry out the project.

Joe called the stout boy, who agreed to meet him at the dock in fifteen minutes. When the young detective drove up, he noticed that the motorcycle was not in the shed. He parked and hurried over to Chet, who was leaning against the boathouse.

"The *Sleuth's* not here," Chet reported.

Joe felt a chill of apprehension. He looked anxiously toward the bay.

"What's the matter?" asked his friend.

Quickly Joe explained that Frank had taken the speedboat and followed the thin man. "But if Sweeper came back and picked up the motorcycle, why didn't Frank return too?"

Chet straightened up. "I don't know," he said uneasily. "It sure doesn't look good."

CHAPTER X

The Deserted Boat

"I've got to find Frank!" Joe said tensely. "This guy Sweeper is an ugly customer."

"What do you think happened?" asked Chet, looking worried.

"I don't know." Joe bit his lip and thought for a moment. "I'd like to borrow a boat and start combing the bay and the coves right now, but there must be a quicker way."

Both boys thought of what might be happening to Frank while they were powerless to help him.

"We've got to do something," said Chet.

"I know! Listen, Chet, you go out in the skiff and look for the floats we planted in the reservoir. Meanwhile, I'll go to police headquarters. Maybe they've had news of Frank."

Chet agreed and twenty minutes later Joe had told his story in Chief Collig's office.

"No," said the stern-faced man. "We've heard nothing.

Joe's heart sank. "I thought maybe the harbor police or the Coast Guard might have found out if something—well, really bad had happened."

Chief Collig shook his head. "This is not like you, Joe." He had known both the Hardys for years and respected the boys' ability as much as their father's. "You don't usually worry until you're sure there's something to worry about."

"But this time I have a hunch," Joe protested.

"You realize that Frank may still be chasing Kimball and someone else might have taken the motorcycle."

"I thought of that," Joe admitted.

The chief said he would alert his men to look for the motorcycle. Later would be time enough to alert the Coast Guard and harbor police.

"Your brother can usually take care of himself," Chief Collig added with a smile. "Go home and wait. He may turn up."

But at nightfall Frank was still missing. Chet telephoned to say that he had found no sign of the wooden objects in the bay. "And the *Sleuth* isn't back yet," he added anxiously. "Is there anything I can do?"

"Thanks, I don't think so," Joe replied. "Luckily Mother and Aunt Gertrude have gone out to dinner and a concert, so I don't have to worry them yet."

Fenton Hardy arrived home about ten o'clock. "Hello, son," he said briskly. "You'll be interested to know that it's possible our wayward plumber is still in Bayport!"

The detective went on to say that he had been to the railroad station, bus terminal, and airport. "No one remembers seeing him so he may still be here. Unless, of course, he left by car. And, another thing," he continued as he took off his jacket and hung it in the hall closet, "I've traced that telegram from Chicago. It's from a member of a small but powerful crime syndicate." Mr. Hardy's voice crackled with anticipation. "I've had leads on the outfit now and then, but this time I may be able to clean up the whole gang. The telegraph office has given Chicago police a clue to the syndicate headquarters. As soon as they—"

"Dad," Joe broke in anxiously.

Mr. Hardy turned and noticed the worried look on Joe's face. "Is anything wrong?"

"I'm afraid so, Dad." He told about Frank's disappearance.

Fenton Hardy was alarmed. "We'll go right now to search the bay!" he declared.

"Frank can't have gone very far in the *Sleuth*," Joe said, "because he didn't have a full tank of fuel."

"I'll ask the harbor police to take us out in their helicopter," his father said.

A two-hour search over Barmet Bay and its coves failed to reveal any sign of the missing boy or of the *Sleuth*. Then the helicopter headed out over deeper water. Every ship in the harbor was signaled, every flickering light and unusual sound investigated. There was no trace of Frank. The pilot looked grim and said nothing, but the police sergeant beside him spoke up. "I'm afraid we're in for some weather. We can't stay up much longer."

"I understand," said Mr. Hardy. "How much time do we have?"

The sergeant looked doubtful. "Don't know. We'll play it by ear."

The Hardys could feel the wind buffeting the light craft with increasing force. The sky was black and starless.

Suddenly the radio in the helicopter crackled and began squawking a message. Joe and his father strained to make out the words over the noise of the motor.

The pilot listened intently and replied "Roger!"

"What did they say?" Joe asked anxiously.

"Headquarters has had a report from an airliner of wreckage on the coast at Land's End. We'll buzz out there and investigate."

Joe did not dare look at his father. Both had the same fear.

In tense silence they stared out the windows

of the craft, straining their eyes to see through the darkness.

"Land's End!" said the sergeant finally. He pointed ahead at a long, dark spit of rocks which thrust out into the sea. White spray dashed high around it.

Moments later the helicopter's searchlight picked out a large fragment of a boat wedged among the rocks. There was no sign of life anywhere.

"It's a speedboat, all right," the sergeant said.

Joe's throat tightened. "I can't see if it's the *Sleuth*," he said.

"Can you go lower?" Mr. Hardy asked the pilot.

"I can't set 'er down," the man replied. "The water's too rough. I'll go as close as I can." He dropped the whirlybird down and kept the light trained on the wreckage.

Joe's heart sank. The broken boat looked like the *Sleuth*. Then suddenly a huge wave crashed over the wreck and part of it broke free. As the wood swirled in the surf, Joe spotted letters on it.

With a surge of relief he exclaimed, "No! It's not ours! Her name's the *Mary Anne*."

Mr. Hardy gave a sigh of relief.

"*Mary Anne!*" exclaimed the sergeant. "So we found her at last! That's the speedboat which was swept away from her moorings in the last big storm we had. Luckily there was nobody aboard."

The pilot reported the discovery into his radio

as he turned the helicopter back toward the bay. The Hardys resumed their watch, but in vain.

"I'm sorry, sir," the pilot told Mr. Hardy at last. "I'm afraid it doesn't look good."

"And we can't keep this 'bird' out much longer," the sergeant said. "The storm's getting worse." He suggested that they search again in daylight and Mr. Hardy said they would.

"Let's try just one more place," Joe pleaded. "Merriam Island."

The sergeant looked skeptical. "If your brother were there," he said, "the lighthouse keeper would have radioed the shore."

"Frank may be there without the keeper's knowledge," Joe persisted. "He could be lying hurt somewhere on the island."

The pilot and sergeant exchanged looks. "It's not much out of the way," Joe urged.

"Okay," the pilot conceded. "But we've got to make it snappy."

He headed seaward again and soon the searchers sighted the windswept, wave-lashed mass of rocks directly ahead of them. The helicopter came down on its pontoons in the shelter of a rock cove. Joe jumped into the shallow water and waded to the narrow, sandy beach. "Look!" he shouted.

The revolving beam of the lighthouse's powerful navigation light had exposed the white hull of the *Sleuth!* The speedboat lay alongside a tiny dock. Joe made his way toward it.

A grizzled, white-haired old man wearing a turtleneck sweater leaned down over the rail of the tall lighthouse's circular runway. He put a megaphone to his lips.

"Who are ye? What do ye want?" he shouted.

"I'm looking for my brother!" Joe yelled.

The lighthouse keeper shook his head. "What?" he roared.

Joe cupped his hands so that his voice would carry over the pounding surf. "I'm looking for my brother!" he shouted again.

"He's not here!" the keeper yelled. "There's nobody on this island but me!"

"He must be here!" Joe shouted. "His boat is moored at the dock!"

He pointed to the boat, and saw the keeper look in that direction. Then the old man shrugged. "Not here!" he repeated, and went inside the lighthouse.

Joe turned to see his father, who had waded to him. "I don't like this at all," Mr. Hardy said.

"Dad, maybe Frank went away on another boat!" Joe suggested. "If he did, he may have left a note!"

The two waded over to the *Sleuth* and examined it carefully. In the cockpit they found Frank's shoes and jacket. The gas tank registered empty. Quickly Joe searched the places he thought Frank might have hidden a note.

"Here's something!" he exclaimed.

Jammed into the short-wave set was a folded piece of white paper! While Mr. Hardy held a flashlight, Joe opened the note. It was from Frank!

The police sergeant came over to them. "Are you almost finished here, sir?" he asked the detective anxiously.

"Officer, my son and I will return to Bayport in the speedboat, if you can lend us some of your spare gasoline!"

"We'll be glad to," the sergeant answered, "but that's likely to be a dangerous trip."

"My son is a skilled pilot," Mr. Hardy said calmly. "Besides, this way we might spot a clue to Frank's whereabouts which we missed from the air."

"We'll be okay," said Joe. "The *Sleuth's* ridden out some rough seas before now."

The sergeant went back to the helicopter and returned with containers of fuel for the *Sleuth*.

"Thanks very much for your assistance," Mr. Hardy told the sergeant. "I'll let you know if we find Frank."

The officer wished them luck, touched his cap, and waded out to the police craft. Joe and his father watched the whirlybird as it rose from the water, then headed toward Bayport, its lights blinking in the darkness.

They reread Frank's brief message: "Going to Sweeper's—"

Why hadn't Frank completed the message? Had he been in too much of a hurry? Or had he been interrupted? And why had he taken off his shoes and jacket?

The two detectives looked out at the wind-whipped, murky water as if it held the answer.

CHAPTER XI

Cast Adrift

WHEN FRANK swung the *Sleuth* out of the boat-house and roared after Sweeper's speeding craft, he knew his mission was a tough one.

"Can't let him know he's being followed," the young detective cautioned himself.

He guided his boat skillfully across Barmet Bay, skirting ships and smaller craft, going fast enough to keep Sweeper in sight without attracting his attention.

The thin man's speedboat headed out to sea. After half an hour Frank saw his quarry approaching rock-bound Merriam Island. Sweeper stowed his boat and disappeared behind a jutting finger of rocks. Frank cut his motor and let the *Sleuth* drift toward a tiny dock which extended from a narrow beach.

He leaped out as his speedboat swung alongside

the dock, and secured it. He saw no sign of activity in the lighthouse tower.

"Guess the keeper's asleep," he muttered.

Staying near the shore, Frank clambered over sharp rocks and ran along short stretches of sand toward the spot where he had seen Sweeper's boat disappear.

Cautiously he approached a cove and saw the craft rocking gently a short distance from land. Sweeper was pacing the beach and glancing frequently out to sea.

"He must be waiting for someone," Frank told himself. To watch the man, he stretched out on a smooth boulder, hidden from Sweeper's view by a low shelf of rocks.

Minutes ticked by. When an hour had passed, Frank saw that Sweeper was becoming impatient. The man paced the sand with short, jerky steps, stopping from time to time to glare at the sea. Finally he rolled up his trouser legs and waded toward his boat.

At that instant came the *put-put* of a launch. It rounded the high rocks sheltering the cove and stopped well beyond the surf.

The man at the wheel fumbled with something in his hands, and tossed a tin can into the water. He waved to Sweeper, pointed at the can, and swung the launch back toward Bayport.

Frank, puzzled, watched the can dance on the waves. Then the surf caught it, and a white lip of foam hurled the container toward the beach.

Sweeper waded out and plucked the can from the water. He pried open the lid and took out a slip of paper. After scanning it, he shook his head, crumpled the paper into a ball, and threw it into the ocean.

The thin man waded to the speedboat, got in, and cast off. A few seconds later he eased his craft out of the cove and sent it roaring through the waves.

Frank rose from his hiding place, ran to the sandy beach, and waded into the surf. He snatched the soggy ball of paper from the churning water. Returning to the beach, he unfolded the dripping sheet carefully. The typewritten message was still legible. It read:

> Meeting postponed until midnight to-night. Will meet you at buoy off Barmet light.

Frank looked across the water. A hundred yards offshore a buoy bobbed. "That must be the one!" he thought, then glanced at his wrist watch. He still had time to return to Bayport and be back to spy on the meeting!

"Wonder who sent Sweeper the message," Frank mused as he made his way back to the *Sleuth*. He cast off the mooring line, climbed into the cockpit, and backed the sleek craft away from the dock.

It was not long, however, before the *Sleuth*'s motor began to sputter. Frank looked quickly at the gas gauge and saw that the fuel was nearly gone. Instantly he headed back toward the island. The motor coughed into silence as the *Sleuth* swung alongside the dock.

Frank tried to radio home for fuel, but found his short-wave set was dead. "What a break!" he muttered.

After working over the equipment for several hours without success, he realized he would have to use the lighthouse radio.

"No use attracting attention to my presence before the meeting here," he decided. "I'll contact the keeper afterward. It'll be easier to spy on Sweeper's boat if I swim out to it."

Frank sat in the cockpit and waited until red streaks of sunset flamed across the sky. Dusk fell and the island grew dark. Frank dozed.

Suddenly he was jarred awake. A motor!

Alert, Frank stared into the darkness in the direction of the sound. In the distance he saw the red and green running lights of an approaching speedboat.

Frank noticed then that the time was twenty minutes to twelve. "Wow!" he exclaimed. "I'd better hurry!"

He got a pencil and a scrap of paper and addressed a note to Joe and his father, in case they should trace him to Merriam Island.

"Going to Sweeper's—" Frank wrote hastily. At that moment the pencil point broke.

Annoyed, Frank searched for another pencil, but gave up after a few moments and jammed the partly written message into the short-wave set.

Swiftly Frank removed his jacket and shoes, then dived cleanly into the water and struck out for the buoy.

The surf was rough and he gasped as the cold waves broke over his head. Settling into a steady crawl, Frank swam toward the blinking light on the buoy.

After a hard swim, he reached it and grabbed hold of an iron chain which dipped deep into the water.

Moments later the speedboat swung past the buoy, coming to a stop. A dinghy was tied behind it. Sweeper stepped to the speedboat's deck and Frank could see that he was looking around.

Watching the man, Frank swam quietly toward the dinghy. As Sweeper's attention turned to an approaching launch, Frank drew himself stealthily into the dinghy. He stretched out on the bottom of the boat. His hand touched a tarpaulin and he pulled the canvas over him.

Wood scraped wood as the launch came alongside the speedboat. Frank lifted a corner of the tarpaulin and peered at the strange craft.

Two men emerged from its cabin and stepped

into the speedboat. One was a stranger. The other Kleng!

They sat with Sweeper in the cockpit of the speedboat and the three began to talk earnestly. Frank strained to hear what they were saying, but the sound of the waves washing against the boats and the tinkle of the bell on the buoy drowned out their words.

Frank inched toward the bow of the dinghy and felt cautiously for the painter that held it to the speedboat. Pulling on it, he brought the small craft near the one which held the three conspirators.

The boy could hear their voices distinctly now. He slid under the tarpaulin once more.

The stranger was speaking. "Alibis! That's all I hear. The syndicate wants action!"

"We need more time," said Kleng.

"Time for what?" the first man snapped. "For those engineers to fill the valley with water and ruin our plans? For Carpenter's detectives to make trouble?"

Frank grinned as Sweeper retorted, "They're just kids! I'll take care of them!"

"See that you do!" the first man told him gruffly. "Kleng, I'll give you four more days! If Foster hasn't completed his tests by that time—"

He broke off as a rattle of tin came from the dinghy. "What's that?" he demanded.

Frank suppressed an exclamation of annoyance. His foot had knocked over an oil can, and it rattled from one side of the boat to the other with every roll of the waves!

"Sounds like a tin can," Kleng remarked.

"I'll get rid of it," Sweeper said. "That racket makes me nervous."

Frantically, Frank felt with his foot, found the can, and pressed it against the side of the dinghy. The rattle stopped.

"Never mind, Sweeper," the stranger said.

Frank breathed in relief until he heard the thin man say softly, "I'm not sure it was just a can. I didn't pull this dinghy right up to the boat, and it didn't drift up! And I didn't spread canvas all over the bottom of it!"

He walked toward the dinghy, bent over its bow, and yanked off the tarpaulin. "Okay, kid!" he snarled. "Get up! The hide-and-seek game's over!"

As Frank stood up, he cast a quick glance toward Merriam Island. His heart sank. The boats had drifted out from the buoy too far for him to swim to safety.

Sweeper turned to the stranger and declared, "This is one of the snoopers who's helping Carpenter and Ames!"

The stranger stared at the youth. Kleng spoke up harshly. "I know this kid. Too smart for

Frank plunged headlong into the sea

his own good. I'll take care of him this time."

The stranger's hand shot out and pulled Kleng back. "No rough stuff," he ordered.

"Let's cut the kid adrift," Sweeper suggested. "The tide's going out. By the time anybody picks him up, we'll be through with our job."

The stranger nodded. "Good idea. Cut the line, Sweeper!"

The thin man removed a pair of oars from the dinghy, then stepped back into the speedboat and unhooked the painter. The dinghy drifted away rapidly.

"So long, kid!" Sweeper called mockingly. "Don't get your feet wet!"

Frank sat down in the boat and watched helplessly as the tide carried it out to sea. He scanned the water. No ship was in sight.

"You've done it now!" he told himself bitterly. "No oars, no food, no water to drink—and if I know anything about clouds, a storm's blowing up!"

Frank studied the water and the black sky. Then, as his eyes fell on the empty oarlocks, a plan formed in his mind.

He straightened the tarpaulin. Then he twisted and squeezed a corner of the canvas to make a short length of rope, which he thrust through one of the locks. He tied the end into a tight knot, tugging it hard against the oarlock to make sure it could not slip through. He did the same with the adjacent corner of the canvas, knotting it outside the second oarlock.

Frank sat and waited as the boat bobbed in the darkness. It was not long before the sea began to churn harder. The wind was rising.

Now Frank stood in front of a seat, holding aloft the untied corners of the tarpaulin. He stretched his arms wide. The impact of the wind rushing into the canvas almost knocked him overboard, but he braced the calves of his legs on the edge of the seat and stiffened himself against the wind and cold water.

The improvised sail sent the boat plunging through the waves toward the island. Lightning snaked across the sky. Thunder boomed and rain fell in torrents. The waves leaped higher and Frank nearly lost his balance several times.

Suddenly a gust of wind caught him full force, tearing a corner of the canvas from his hands. He reached for the flapping tarpaulin, but lost his footing just as a huge wave sent the dinghy reeling. Frank pitched forward and plunged headlong into the sea.

The boy struggled to the surface and shook the water from his eyes. The dinghy was drifting away rapidly, whipped by the wind!

CHAPTER XII

Decoy Hunt

DESPERATELY, Frank's eyes searched the darkness for the island. A wave lifted him, and he was suddenly conscious of the tinkling of a bell.

The buoy!

He turned his head and saw the light a few feet from him, bobbing and blinking. Thankfully, Frank swam toward it and clung to the chain. The island was only a hundred yards away, but his strength was gone. He closed his eyes and waited for the storm to abate.

It was daylight when the weather cleared. Frank attempted to strike out for the sandy shore. But his arms felt too heavy to move.

Suddenly he spotted a helicopter approaching the island.

Frank shouted and waved weakly. He saw a man signal through the craft's window, and a minute later the helicopter hovered directly over him and started to descend.

It halted thirty feet above the water and hung in the air. The cabin door was thrust open and a blond-haired youth looked down.

"Frank!" he yelled. "Hang on! We'll drop a line!"

It was Joe! Frank grinned. "I'm all right!" he yelled as loudly as he could. "Just get me out of this soup!"

Joe laughed with relief. "Okay!" he called. "Catch!" A nylon rescue line with a breeches buoy was dropped, and Frank was drawn up safely into the helicopter.

"Boy! I was afraid for a minute I was seeing things!" Frank said weakly as his brother and father wrapped him in blankets.

Frank did not feel strong enough to discuss his experience until he was home and had taken a hot shower. Then, fortified with a bowl of hearty soup, he described in detail what had happened.

Mrs. Hardy and Aunt Gertrude looked worried. "It's a wonder you didn't drown!" his aunt declared. "I think a doctor should have a look at you." Frank insisted he felt much better.

"But you must be exhausted," his mother said. "I think you should get right into bed." Mr. Hardy agreed.

"I am pretty tired," Frank confessed with a smile. As Joe accompanied his brother upstairs, he told him of his discovery that Sweeper was Timothy Kimball Jr.

"I thought Sweeper was a phony-sounding name," Frank said, smothering a yawn.

"Or a nickname," Joe said.

But Frank had already stretched out on his bed and was beginning to doze. Joe tiptoed from the room and found his father waiting for him in the study.

"What Frank overheard last night means we'll have to act fast," Mr. Hardy said quietly. "I'm afraid of what the gang will do to Dr. Foster. If only we knew where they're holding him!"

"My guess is that they have a hideout on Skull Mountain," Joe said. "He may be there. If we could find Kleng or Sweeper, we might be able to follow them to the place."

"Right," said Fenton Hardy. "Joe, you go to Kleng's house. Try to find out if he's there—if not, when he'll be back. And, son—be careful."

"I understand," Joe told him.

"The plumbing shop is closed," Mr. Hardy went on, "but Kleng and the others may be using it as a meeting place. Do you suppose Chet could stand watch on it? The crooks would be less apt to notice a boy than a man, I think."

"Sure, Chet could do it," Joe said.

"Good!" The tall detective put on his hat. "I'm going to Brookside and see if I can get Mr.

Kimball to talk. He might know something that would help us."

Joe phoned Chet and told him of Frank's rescue. The stout boy was relieved. He quickly agreed to stake out the shop. Then he paused. "Oh!"

"What's the matter?" Joe said.

"I asked Biff Hooper to meet me at the boat landing this morning. I decided it would be easier for two people to look for those wooden things—one could man the boat if the water got rough."

Joe debated for a moment. "You'd better go ahead with that plan," he decided. "The markers may come through the tunnel any time. I'll watch Kleng's house and later take over in the bay, while you keep an eye on the plumbing shop."

"Check," his friend agreed.

The window shades were still drawn in Kleng's house when Joe drove up. He stepped onto the porch and rang the doorbell. To his surprise, the door opened at once and a middle-aged woman wearing a faded dressing gown faced him. "What d'ya want?"

"Mrs. Kleng?" Joe asked politely.

"Yeah."

"Is your husband at home?" Joe asked.

"No." The woman regarded Joe suspiciously. "What d'ya want him for?"

"Our kitchen faucet is leaking," Joe told her. "We need someone to fix it."

The woman smirked. "It'll make a pool if you wait for Kleng to take care of it. He's away on a trip."

"Oh, that's right," said Joe, as if he suddenly remembered where the man had gone. "Did he take a boat?"

"Boat?" the woman asked. "You don't go to the hills by—" She broke off abruptly and slammed the door in the boy's face.

Joe grinned as he ran down the steps. The woman had been caught off guard. So Kleng was in the hills. That must mean Skull Mountain!

Joe drove to the boathouse. He guided the *Sleuth* out of her slip and headed into the bay. A short distance from shore he saw Chet sitting in the skiff with Biff Hooper, a high school companion.

"Hi!" Joe called. The two waved to him, and Joe brought the *Sleuth* alongside the skiff.

"See anything yet?" Joe asked eagerly.

Chet shook his head. "Maybe the stuff got stuck somewhere in the tunnel," he said. "How'd you do at Kleng's house?"

Joe told him. Chet grinned and said, "Boy, you did good! I hope I find out something at the plumbing shop."

"Want me to go out in the *Sleuth* with you now?" Biff asked Joe.

"I wish you would, two pairs of eyes are better than one. And Chet had better head for his stake-out."

"Fine," said Biff. "I've fished for everything else in these waters. I may as well try my luck at catching a decoy duck!"

Joe towed the skiff back to the boathouse and moored it there. Chet stepped ashore and saluted importantly. "Detective Morton on duty!" he announced, and hurried away.

Chet found the plumbing shop closed, as Mr. Hardy had said. The stout boy peered through the plate-glass window, but saw no one inside.

Directly across the street was a hot-dog stand. Chet brightened.

"Chow time!" he exulted. "Twelve o'clock!" Besides, he could station himself by the stand. Nobody would suspect he was watching.

Chet strode over and ordered a hot dog and a tall glass of orange juice.

Two frankfurters and three glasses of juice later, Chet was still waiting for some sign of action at Kleng's shop.

For an hour he strolled up and down the street keeping an eye on the store. Finally he stopped at the stand again and ordered a doughnut. As he took it from the man, he turned to face the store again. Suddenly his eyes widened.

A man was unlocking the door of the plumbing shop!

Chet gulped nervously as the man limped into the store. Thrusting the doughnut into his pocket, the stout boy crossed the street. He looked through the window, but could not see anyone.

The young detective wet his lips, and his Adam's apple bobbed as he swallowed. He tried the door and found it locked. Wiping his forehead, Chet paced back and forth for several minutes, staying a short distance from the shop.

Suddenly he started. Two men were leaving Kleng's place! Backing into a doorway, Chet watched them cross the street. One was the man with the limp. The other was tall and thin.

As the pair neared the opposite curb, the taller man glanced around as if he suspected they were being followed. Chet swallowed and tried to look as if he were examining his wrist watch. The two men mounted a motorcycle and roared away.

Chet's eyes popped at the peculiar, uneven rhythm of the motor. It was the machine Frank and Joe had described!

"Well, I guess I cased them!" Chet said to himself. "Now to report to headquarters!"

At the Hardys' house, Chet found Mr. Hardy and Frank seated in the detective's study. After greeting them, Chet earnestly told of his vigil. He wiped his brow as he concluded, "It was touch and go for a few minutes!"

Mr. Hardy smiled, but declared heartily, "That's good work, Chet!"

"Are you going to tell the police?" the stout boy asked eagerly. "They could find the motorcycle and follow it to see where those fellows go!"

"That's too risky," replied Mr. Hardy. "If the gang got wind of the police, they might silence Dr. Foster and clear out fast. There's a little time yet," he added. "We must find them quietly on our own, then bring in help." The detective went on to tell his visit to Brookside. "I persuaded Mr. Kimball to level with me. Actually he doesn't know as much as we do."

"What about the man with the limp?" Chet asked.

Mr. Hardy shrugged. "A confederate. I feel sure now it would pay us to post a regular watch on the plumbing shop."

Chet asked, "You mean me?"

"Why not?" the detective queried. "You did a good job today!"

The boy beamed. "Leave it to me, Mr. Hardy!"

Frank stood up. "Dad says Joe is watching Kleng's house."

"No, he was there," said Chet, and told what Joe had found out about the plumber.

"He's gone to Skull Mountain, all right," said Frank, "and that's where we should go to search for that hideout."

"You can start tomorrow," his father agreed. "Where's Joe now, Chet?"

"Out in the *Sleuth* with Biff Hooper. They're looking for the stuff we planted in the reservoir."

"I'll go down and help them," said Frank. "Coming, Chet?"

"You bet."

It was late afternoon when the boys arrived at the boathouse. The *Sleuth* had not returned.

"We'll use our rowboat to look for Joe and Biff," Frank said.

They found the *Sleuth* anchored in the bay. Joe and Biff were sitting in the cockpit. Frank rowed alongside. "Any luck?" he asked.

"No," his brother replied. "I'm afraid the stuff came through during the storm and was washed out to sea."

"If so," Frank said, frowning, "we'll have to forget it for now. First thing in the morning we've got to go to Skull Mountain and search for Dr. Foster."

The Hardys swapped places, Frank taking the wheel of the *Sleuth,* Joe joining Chet in the rowboat. They hooked it by a towline to the speedboat and started off. Frank guided the two crafts as close to the rocky shore as he dared.

The boys examined the numerous coves which bit into the shoreline of the bay. Hours later, when it was dark, they still had seen no sign of the markers.

"Let's quit," Chet pleaded. "I'm starved!"

"We'll try one more cove," Frank said. "If we don't spot the things, we'll go home."

He steered the *Sleuth* toward a rocky slit in the shore, then cut the motor. The two boats drifted into the cove.

Frank trained the speedboat's searchlight on the steep shore. As he swept the light slowly along the water line, the other youths searched with their flashlights.

The lights made a complete sweep around the cove, but the boys saw nothing in the water.

Discouraged, Frank swung his craft slowly back toward the mouth of the inlet.

Suddenly Joe thought he saw a small white object bump against the *Sleuth* and veer away. "Hold it!" he yelled.

Frank quickly cut the motor and Joe leaned over the bow of the rowboat. He aimed the beam of his flashlight at the water.

With a whoop of joy he reached down and held up a dripping object. "Here it is—our duck!"

CHAPTER XIII

Dangerous Cargo

"THAT DOES IT!" Frank exclaimed as Joe showed the wet decoy to his excited companions. "Now we're sure there's an underground channel from the reservoir to the bay!"

"It must be a rough ride through the tunnel," Biff remarked. "Look at the scratches on that duck!"

"Let's see," Frank said, and Joe passed him the decoy. He examined it carefully. "No clues on this, but it gives me an idea. Let's look for the barrel stave and pine slab. Maybe there will be something on them to show where they entered the channel."

Using the *Sleuth's* searchlight, the boys scanned the surface of the water, but found nothing more.

"I bet the rest of the things are stuck somewhere in the tunnel," Chet said.

Biff peered over the side of the speedboat.

"Must be a current down below," he observed. "Look how roily the water is here."

Frank nodded. "It's probably the fresh water flowing in from the reservoir—and stirring up the sand and mud particles on the bottom of the cove."

The Hardys decided to return at daylight to see if the stave or slab had come through. Frank pressed the *Sleuth's* starter button, and the motor throbbed. Before he eased the two boats carefully out of the cove, Joe took a piece of white chalk from his pocket and inscribed a large X on a rock, well above the high-tide mark.

At dawn the Hardys returned and easily found the chalk-marked cove again.

As Frank guided the *Sleuth* into the inlet, Joe grinned and pointed to a red-and-white object whirling in the water. "How's that for luck!" he exclaimed.

Frank eased the craft over and Joe seized the barrel stave.

Quickly they examined it. Stuck in the cracked wood was a twig of bramble bush!

"That's our clue!" Frank exclaimed. "There can't be bramble in the underground channel, so this twig must have caught on the stave as it was swept into the opening."

Joe chuckled. "Now all we have to do is locate the right bramble bush and we'll know where the entrance to the tunnel is."

Elated at their discovery, the boys headed the *Sleuth* back to the boathouse. The fresh breeze cutting across the bay aroused their appetites.

"I could eat a stack of flapjacks," Joe said as they stepped ashore.

"So could I. With sausages."

As the boys were crossing the boat landing on their way to a nearby diner, Frank suddenly clutched Joe by the arm. "Do you see what I see?" he whispered, pulling his brother down with him behind an empty barrel.

Walking along the dock was Sailor Hawkins! The old sea dog's back was toward the boys, but his short, squat figure and rolling gait were immediately familiar.

"What do you suppose he's doing in Bayport?" asked Joe.

Frank shook his head. "One of us had better follow him," he said. "He may be on some business for Sweeper."

"I'll do it," Joe told him. "You drive home and pick up the stuff we'll need for the camp. I'll phone you later and tell you where to meet me."

Joe followed Hawkins down the dock to a loading platform. He kept his eyes on the sailor, while side-stepping the shouting, sweating longshoremen who were trundling barrels and crates onto the wharf.

The arm of a boom swung out from a freighter over the loading platform and hooked a rope net laden with heavy boxes. The cable drew taut and the net was hauled swiftly into the air.

"Look out!" a dockhand yelled frantically.

Joe's head snapped up at the warning. One of the rope strands had broken, and the hook had torn loose from the net. The heavy cargo was hurtling down on him.

He flung himself to one side and the boxes crashed to the dock—not six feet away! There was a surge of excited voices as men looked down at him from the rail of the freighter while others ran toward him along the wharf.

A longshoreman helped the youth to his feet. "Are you hurt?" he asked.

Joe shook his head and brushed the dirt from his clothes. He looked at the spot where he had last seen Hawkins, but the sailor had disappeared.

With quick thanks, Joe shook off the dockhand and made his way toward the row of supply houses, cheap restaurants, and second-hand stores which lined the street opposite the wharf.

He looked through the windows of the stores, but did not see Sailor Hawkins.

Finally, at the end of the row, Joe came to a large warehouse. Cautiously he stepped inside. The dim interior was stacked with crates, but there were no longshoremen in sight. Joe stopped short. Not far away on a box sat Hawkins! His head was bent as he lit an old corncob pipe.

Joe slipped behind a large crate and waited.

Soon he heard uneven footsteps approaching along the wooden floor. From his hiding place, he could make out a small, furtive-looking man who walked with a limp!

Joe tingled with sudden excitement. During the search for the outlet in the bay, Chet had told of seeing a man with Sweeper whose description tallied with this stranger's.

The limping man went straight to the sailor and they exchanged a few whispered words. Then the small man took some bills from his wallet, counted them carefully, and gave the money to Hawkins.

"For the food," he said aloud.

At that moment a dockworker came pushing a hand truck through the warehouse door. He stared curiously at the two men, then moved the truck toward the crate which concealed Joe.

"Oh no!" Joe thought. "Not this one!"

The laborer tilted the crate and slid the shoe of the truck under it. Joe glanced helplessly at the nearest place of concealment. It was the stack of crates beside which Hawkins and the limping stranger were standing.

An instant later the longshoreman saw the boy. "Hey!" he demanded. "What are you doing here?"

Hawkins and the stranger turned swiftly. "So it's you!" the old sailor roared, taking a threatening step toward Joe. "You blasted little spy!"

The limping man grabbed the sailor's arm. "No, Hawkins!"

He whispered something rapidly in the seaman's ear. Then the two men separated. Hawkins ran out the front door of the warehouse, while the man with the limp made for the rear exit.

Joe swerved past the dockworker and raced after Hawkins. The old sea dog's short legs carried him with surprising speed, but Joe was more than a match for him.

He saw the sailor dodge into a doorway. Joe quickly stepped behind a truck. After a moment he saw Hawkins peer out from his refuge. Satisfied that he had shaken off his pursuer, the seaman walked calmly along the row of stores and entered a self-service grocery.

Joe went to the window of the store and stealthily looked in. Hawkins was going slowly up one of the aisles, selecting groceries.

"He'll be there for a while," Joe thought, noticing that a long line was waiting at the single check-out counter. The boy hurried into a drugstore and telephoned Frank.

"Meet me as soon as you can," Joe instructed his brother and recounted his adventure. "Hawkins is buying a big load of supplies. They must be for the gang up on the mountain!"

When Joe hung up, Frank relayed the information to their father. "Maybe we can follow Hawkins to the hideout!" the boy said as he slipped into his jacket.

"I'd go with you," said Mr. Hardy, "but I've had a call from the Chicago police asking me to stand by. I'll have to go there as soon as they're certain they've located the syndicate headquarters." He reminded Frank to be cautious and added, "Good luck, son!"

Frank dashed to the convertible, which was already packed with their gear, and drove to the grocery.

"Hawkins loaded the supplies into an old jalopy and left five minutes ago," Joe said as he hopped into the seat beside Frank.

A few miles out of Bayport on the highway leading toward Skull Mountain the boys saw a dilapidated sedan ahead of them.

"That's the car!" Joe exclaimed.

Frank let the convertible slow down and adjusted its speed to the sedan's rattling pace.

Soon the old car turned off onto the same dirt road the boys had used to detour the landslide. Frank and Joe followed at a distance. At the foot of the narrow trail which mounted the slope to the ridge, the sedan stopped. Quickly Frank parked the convertible behind a clump of trees.

A man the boys had never seen came out of the

brush and helped Hawkins lift the heavy crate from the sedan. Together they started to carry it up the path.

The Hardys waited until Hawkins and his companion had a good head start, then followed. The men stopped frequently to rest, but finally reached the top of the mountain and disappeared behind a clump of boulders.

Frank and Joe quickly climbed the last steep section of the trail and cautiously rounded the same rocks. They stopped short, staring in surprise at a large empty clearing.

The stocky sailor and his helper had vanished!

CHAPTER XIV

A Mountain Puzzle

"WHAT happened to them?" Joe asked.

Frank shook his head. "It beats me," he replied. "I don't see where two men could have gone so quickly—especially carrying that heavy box."

In the clearing where Frank and Joe stood there were only a few patches of blueberry bushes as high as the boys' knees. The rest of the mountaintop was covered with trees. The brothers searched the woods, but found no trace of Hawkins or his companion.

"Come on!" Joe said impatiently. "This is getting us nowhere."

They started down the mountain toward the reservoir, and half an hour later arrived at the camp. Bob and Dick greeted them with enthusiasm. It took the boys a full hour to recount their adventures and discoveries since they had last seen the engineers.

"By the way," Joe said, "you were absolutely right about the subterranean channel."

Bob and Dick exchanged looks of astonishment. "How do you know?" Bob asked. "We're supposed to be the experts here, and you're not giving us a chance!" He grinned.

Frank explained the boys' experiment. "The gang must have devised a way to drain the water off at will," he added. "That's why it happens only at night."

"And naturally when it's dark," Joe put in, "it would make it tougher to trace the current."

"But we have a clue that may help you," Frank said, and told of the bramble twig.

"Fellows, you're great!" Bob exclaimed. "I'll put the sounding crew to work looking for the bramble patch." He went on to say that the new electronic equipment would not arrive until the next day, because it was coming from New York. "The water shortage is getting worse," he added soberly. "We've just got to find that outlet!"

"And Joe and I have to locate the hideout and Dr. Foster," Frank said. "You know," he went on thoughtfully, "the gang must have some kind of equipment in the tunnel to shut the water off. If we find the channel, we might catch one of the gang members in there and make him talk."

"That's an idea!" said Joe. "Let's concentrate today on finding the channel opening. Too bad Chet's staked out at Kleng's shop," he added. "We could use him!"

After lunch the four set out. Bob and Dick circled the reservoir in the rowboat while the Hardys and the six-man crew walked along the shore to investigate the slopes above the present water line.

Hour after hour passed as the group inspected the banks, prodding and tearing with long poles, sticks and hatchets in an attempt to expose the earth wherever they found patches of brambles.

The prickly foliage clung to the rocky slope, scratching the boys' hands and ankles when they dug into the underbrush.

"I have a feeling we've been through this before!" Joe said gloomily.

Late in the afternoon the four returned to the camp for a quick supper, but resumed their work at the reservoir immediately afterward. As dusk settled over the valley, the water level began to drop noticeably.

Suddenly Frank gripped Joe's arm and pointed toward the crest of Skull Mountain, still bathed in a clear, yellow light. "Look!" he exclaimed. "The smoke again!"

Joe gazed at it intently for a few moments. "It looks to me as though it's coming from the clearing where Hawkins and his pal disappeared so suddenly."

"You're right!" Frank said.

Bob and Dick were still in the rowboat. The Hardys shouted that they would join the engineers later, and started up the hillside. Darkness closed in around them as they climbed toward the steady stream of smoke.

"I've got a pocket flashlight," said Frank, "but we'd better not use it. No telling who may be around here."

"I hope that fire's still burning when we get there." Joe grunted. "I've run up and down this hill so often I feel like a mountain goat!"

No sooner had he spoken than the column of smoke vanished.

"That does it!" Joe declared in disgust.

"Come on!" Frank urged. "We've almost reached the top. It would be foolish to turn back now."

Clambering over rocks in the darkness, the brothers finally arrived at the treeless patch on the summit.

"Not a trace of smoke," said Joe.

"We'll wait," Frank decided. "If it starts up again, we'll be here to spot it."

The boys made themselves comfortable on the ground. Overhead the stars sparkled, and a full moon rose slowly above the hill on the other side of the reservoir. The night air was cool and fresh. As they sat quietly, a figure emerged from the trees beyond the clearing.

Instantly the boys flattened themselves on the ground behind some blueberry bushes. In the moonlight the man looked like a scarecrow.

"There's your hermit, Frank!" exclaimed Joe.

He crossed the clearing and dumped his armful of fresh-cut firewood. After glancing cautiously around, he hurried to the top of the trail and looked down.

Satisfied, the fellow returned to the load of wood he had dropped. He bent and tugged at something nearby, then lifted aside a large, squarish slab of rock.

A narrow cleft showed black in the moonlight! Cradling the wood in his arms, the hermit stepped into the fissure and disappeared!

CHAPTER XV

The Escaping Stream

FRANK AND JOE ran to the spot where the hermit had disappeared. They peered down the dark cleft in the mountaintop. There was no sign of the man.

"This must be the source of the smoke!" Frank declared. "The rock is like a chimney cover."

The two examined the slab and saw that there was a handhold chiseled into the underface so that it could be moved from the inside to close the crevice.

"This made a convenient escape hatch for Hawkins and his pal today!" Frank said.

"It seems to be a tunnel," Joe mused. "Wonder where it goes."

Frank lowered himself to the floor of the cleft. As Joe watched, he tested the slab to see how well it concealed the opening.

"It's perfect!" Joe told him.

Frank seemed puzzled. "But for the smoke to come out, the crack has to be open—and then the cleft could be spotted easily."

"Sure," his brother said. "But who's to see it? Bob and Dick have no business up here. That leaves us, maybe Potato Annie—"

"And Kleng's gang," Frank finished for him.

With his flashlight, Frank stepped down farther into the narrow fissure and shot the beam ahead. A low passage sloped downward into darkness. "You're right! It's a real tunnel!" he declared.

"Let's have a look," Joe said, dropping in beside his brother. He borrowed Frank's light and played it on the irregular walls of the fissure. They were grimy with smoke smudges.

"Let's explore it!" Joe urged.

"Okay. And find out where that hermit went."

One behind the other, the boys crept into the tunnel and crawled slowly downward into the darkness. Here and there the passage turned sharply.

Suddenly Joe's palm came down on a smooth cold object which rolled under his weight. With a startled gasp, he jerked back. The flashlight beam probed ahead, then shone directly on the object. *It was a human skull!*

Joe let out a sigh of relief. "The hermit's trademark!" he whispered.

Frank chuckled softly, and the boys crawled on, with still no sight of the mountain man.

Soon the long, narrow shaft turned sharply again. Joe shot the light ahead, then exclaimed in relief as he inched a few feet forward and stood upright. The passage had become large enough to allow the boys to walk side by side. They did not go far, however, before they were forced to stop.

"The tunnel forks!" Joe said. "Now what do we do? And which way did that hermit go?"

"Let's try the left."

The broad passageway sloped downward, until the Hardys felt sure they had reached the very heart of the mountain. The air was damp but pure, and they breathed it gratefully.

"Wonder where it comes from," Joe thought.

Down and down they went. Suddenly the tunnel leveled off, forming a small landing. Beyond, they could see that the shaft dropped sharply. The boys felt a swift current of air.

Suddenly Joe grabbed Frank's arm. "Listen!" he whispered.

From the depth below came the rush of running water! The boys stepped to the edge of the landing and Joe aimed his light downward.

Flowing through a channel at the foot of the shaft was a swift, bubbling stream. "It's the water from the reservoir!" Frank exclaimed.

"How do you know?"

"It has to be!" Frank told him. "It's flowing from the direction of the valley!"

"Directions don't mean much inside of a mountain," Joe said doubtfully. "When we crawled through that passage, I lost track of which way is which."

"Well, it'll be easy to check," his brother declared. "We'll come back here during the day. If the water isn't flowing then, we'll be pretty certain that the channel runs from the reservoir!"

"Wait till Bob and Dick hear about this!" Joe said. "They'll want to see for themselves."

Frank nodded. "I think we'd better head for camp and tell them about it."

The boys retraced their steps rapidly. When they reached the fork, Joe paused and said, "I'd sure like to know where this right-hand tunnel leads."

"Let's walk in a little way," Frank suggested. "This must be where the hermit went."

About a dozen feet into the passageway, Joe stopped abruptly. "Look!" he said. With his light he pointed to a piece of bark which lay on the ground. "That proves he came this way with his armload of wood!"

"The tunnel must lead to the place where the wood is burned—probably a cavern," Frank said. "I'd be willing to bet that's the gang's headquarters!"

Joe grinned. "Let's pay 'em a surprise visit!"

"The tunnel forks!" Joe said. "Which way did
that hermit go?"

"No," Frank said. "The two of us would be no match for the whole bunch."

"But we could spy on them and find out what their game is," Joe persisted. "We might even find Dr. Foster."

"That's quite possible," Frank agreed. "But if they caught us, it would wreck the whole rescue operation."

Joe saw the point and the boys returned to the place where the tunnel forked and resumed climbing. Soon they dropped to their hands and knees and crawled into the low tunnel which led to the mountaintop. Joe went ahead with the flashlight, Frank following a few feet behind.

The air was thinner and their progress slower. The boys were still some distance from the top when Frank stopped and began to sniff. "Joe—" he called.

"I know. I smell it too."

Rising from the passage below them was the odor of wood smoke!

Joe groaned, remembering the open fissure at the top of the mountain. "We called this a chimney, but we forgot what that means!" he said to himself ruefully.

"Hurry!" Frank urged. "We must get out of here!"

As the boys scrambled upward, the smoke became thicker. It wreathed around them, stinging their eyes and making them cough and gasp for air.

The two crawled on, hoping that each turn in the shaft would bring them to the opening.

Smoke now began to stream through the passage in a dense cloud. The boys clutched at their throats and coughed until they felt their lungs would burst.

Suddenly Frank collapsed. His hands clawed at the rock floor, but his limbs were too heavy to move. The walls of the low tunnel seemed to be closing in on him!

"Keep going, Joe!" he called hoarsely. He heard his own voice as if it were coming from a great distance. "I can't make it!"

He saw Joe turn. Then the flashlight spun out of his brother's hand and the smoke-filled tunnel was plunged into darkness!

CHAPTER XVI

A Night Light

How LONG Frank had been unconscious, he did not know. As he revived, his eyes still smarted from the smoke, but above him he could see a starry sky. A hand tilted a canteen toward his lips and cool water dribbled into his parched mouth.

"Take it easy," a voice said. "You'll be all right."

Frank's eyes opened wide. The speaker was Bob.

"Where—? What—?" Frank began, then remembered. "Joe," he asked anxiously, raising himself on his elbows. "Is he—?"

Bob pushed him down gently. "He's safe, too."

Frank sank back, relieved. "How did you find us?" he asked after a few moments.

"We saw the smoke when you and Joe started up the slope," Bob told him, "and figured you were going to investigate it."

Dick added, "When the smoke disappeared and you didn't return, we came up on the ridge to look for you."

Bob nodded. "We saw the open crevice and crawled in, but didn't go far before smoke started to come up."

"It was lucky we saw your light before it went out," Dick went on. "You weren't far from the mouth of the crevice."

Frank smiled gratefully. Then, as Bob and Dick gave their attention to Joe, Frank looked about him. A short distance away smoke was still pouring from the open fissure.

It was several minutes before Joe regained consciousness. By then Frank had gathered strength. He went to kneel beside his brother.

"Oh, my aching head!" Joe mumbled.

Frank nodded. "Guess that's what happens to people who go exploring in chimneys!"

Soon both boys declared they felt strong enough to make the descent to the camp. They moved slowly, their knees still weak. When the four reached the shack, Frank and Joe told the engineers what they had discovered.

"You've found the channel!" Bob exclaimed. "That's terrific!"

"I think so," said Frank, "and we're pretty sure the gang has headquarters inside that mountain!"

"It sounds possible," Bob agreed. "But why do they want the water to run out of the reservoir?"

"I don't know yet," Frank replied. "But at least we can make sure tomorrow whether the channel is the right one."

"Dick and I will go with you," Bob said promptly. "But first we ought to get gas masks. We don't want to be smoked out in that chimney!"

"There are some gas masks in your office in Bayport," Dick told him. "I stowed 'em there after our last field trip. Guess I'd better drive down and get them."

"We'll do it!" Joe said. He explained that Fenton Hardy must be told of their suspicions about the hideout in the mountain.

Bob gave the boys his office key. "How about hitting the trail first thing in the morning?" he asked.

"Make it at sunup," Frank said. "Joe and I will meet you at the top of the mountain!"

Later, as the boys spun along the highway in their convertible, the cool night air cleared their lungs of the last bit of smoke.

They stopped at Bob's office to pick up oxygen masks, then drove through the streets of Bayport. The usually bustling business section was silent and deserted. It was almost midnight.

As they approached Kleng's shop, Frank slowed the car and the two looked through the plate-glass window. Swiftly Frank brought the convertible to a stop a few feet beyond the store.

A light shone in the rear of the shop! The boys walked stealthily back to the window and saw that the gleam came from a transom over the door of Kleng's office.

Cautiously Joe tried the door of the shop. It was unlocked. He started to open it, but his brother seized his arm.

"Hold it!" he whispered.

Frank looked along the deserted street. In front of a fruit store a few doors away some empty crates had been piled at the curb to be picked up by the rubbish collectors.

He carried the largest crate to the door and stood it on end. Then he climbed onto the box and pushed open the door a few inches with one hand. With the other he stuffed his handkerchief up into the bell, which tinkled every time someone entered the shop.

"It can't give us away now," he whispered to Joe, and pushed the door wide.

After quickly replacing the crate at the curb, the boys slipped into the shop, closing the door quietly behind them.

The door to Kleng's office was closed, but the transom was slightly ajar. The boys could hear a faint murmur of voices.

Frank gestured to Joe, and they tiptoed toward the office. As they came to the end of the counter, they suddenly heard a muffled thumping.

"What was that?" Joe whispered, startled.

The noise came again. The boys leaned over the counter and looked down. Someone was lying on the floor, bound and gagged!

Joe ran around the counter and turned on his flashlight. A pair of eyes looked at him appealingly. The prisoner was Chet Morton!

CHAPTER XVII

The Rear Room

JOE UNTIED the rope which bound Chet's hands and feet, while Frank removed the plump boy's gag.

Chet gasped. "Am I glad—"

"Not so loud!" Frank cautioned him in a low voice, glancing toward the office.

"How did this happen?" Joe asked softly.

In a whisper Chet said that while returning from a late movie, he had decided to pass the plumbing shop to see if everything was in order.

"I saw the light—thought I ought to investigate," he went on. "The bell tinkled when I stepped into the shop and two guys came out of the back room and jumped me."

He looked at the Hardys quizzically. "How come the bell didn't give you away?"

Joe showed his handkerchief and Chet nodded understandingly.

"Who are they?" Frank queried, nodding toward the rear room.

"Sweeper and Limpy."

The three boys looked at the light in the transom over the closed door. Although they could hear voices, the sound was too faint for them to distinguish the words.

Suddenly they became aware of a strange, hissing noise.

Frank tiptoed to the door and looked through the keyhole, but the key was in it. Quietly he placed a chair beside the door, climbed up, and gently pushed open the transom a few more inches.

Sweeper and the man with the limp were kneeling on the floor in front of a small iron safe. Sweeper was holding an acetylene torch, and its bluish flame was cutting a circle through the metal around the lock of the safe.

Frank felt a tug at his trouser leg and looked down. Chet was eager to see what was going on.

Frank stepped down and whispered, "Safe-cracking."

As Chet climbed onto the chair, both Hardys signaled him to be careful.

Chet nodded reassuringly, then tried to peek through the transom. "I can't reach!" he whispered. "Can you find me a couple of books to stand on?"

Joe nodded reluctantly. He brought a few

bound catalogs from the counter and Chet stacked them on the seat of the chair. He climbed onto them and teetered precariously.

"Watch out!" Frank whispered sharply. He grabbed at the plump youth, but too late! Chet gave Frank a wild, despairing look as the catalogs skidded out from under his feet. He leaped to the floor, past the tumbling books.

The boys heard exclamations from inside the office. The acetylene torch was shut off.

Swiftly Frank lifted the chair away from the door, then he and Joe ducked behind the end of a far counter. Chet lay down where he had been before as if bound and jammed the gag into his mouth. The office door was flung open and Sweeper came straight to Chet.

"Mmm. Okay. It wasn't him."

"Then what was it?" asked Limpy from the doorway.

Sweeper stared at the books sprawled near the upright chair. At that moment a large black cat walked into the rectangle of light which streamed through the open doorway. He stopped and looked at the two men, then meowed piteously.

Sweeper laughed. "A snooping cat—that's what it was!" he said, pointing. "Must've jumped on the chair and knocked all those books off."

He picked up a book and threw it at the animal. The cat squalled and ran to another part of the shop.

"Come on, Green!" Sweeper said impatiently. "We've got to finish this job."

Green limped after him and closed the door. Again there came the sound of the acetylene torch.

Frank signaled a huddle, and the boys moved some distance from the door. "We must get word to Dad and Chief Collig."

But Chet shook his head. "Your dad's in Chicago," he whispered. "He got a phone call shortly after you left to pick up Joe at the grocery. He telephoned me and said to tell you he'd be back as soon as he could."

Joe groaned. "And we wanted to show him the tunnel and look for the hideout."

"We'll have to handle it alone," said Frank. He turned to Chet. "The convertible's parked a few doors to the left of the shop. Drive to Chief Collig's house and bring him here!"

"Will do," said Chet, and hurried out.

The Hardys hastened back to the office door and Joe took up the watch. Several minutes later he saw the torch cut a complete circle through the metal of the safe. Its lock fell out onto the floor.

Sweeper swung the heavy door open, reached into the safe, and took out a metal box. He snapped the lid up and dumped the contents on a desk.

The thin man fumbled through some papers

impatiently, then snatched an envelope. He drew out a roll of currency.

"There it is!" he cried exultantly, flipping the bills with his thumb. "Five thousand bucks! Kleng's promised me this cash ever since I started to do his dirty work, but he's never delivered. Well, we're square now, even if Kleng doesn't know it!"

Green wasn't listening. He leafed nervously through the scattered papers, wetting his lips and muttering under his breath.

Finally he drew out a bank check and stared at it. His fingers trembled. A look of triumph came over his face.

"That it?" Sweeper asked.

"Yes." Green looked at Sweeper, his mouth quivering. "For years, Kleng's been holding this against me," he said. "I used to be a respectable accountant. I worked for Kleng. Then, to get more money for my family, I forged his name to this check." He broke off and stared at the slip of paper. "Kleng threatened to have me sent to jail unless I helped him carry out his scheme. But now!" His voice was suddenly gleeful. "I'll destroy the check and be free!"

Sweeper laughed. "We're both free, fella! You can forget Kleng and I'll spend the five thousand!"

Suddenly the boys heard a noise at the front door. Someone outside was fumbling with the handle. Quickly Joe stepped down, swung the chair aside, and ducked behind the counter with Frank.

The front door opened and sharp heel taps sounded on the floor. From their hiding place, the boys saw a woman open the office door. The light fell on her face.

Mrs. Kleng! She stared into the back room. "What are you two doing here?" she demanded.

Then the boys saw Sweeper's arm pull her into the office. The door slammed shut.

Joe glanced at Frank. "What shall we do?"

"Better wait for Chet and the chief. If the three in there try to leave, we'll stop them."

Angry voices sounded in the office. In shrill tones Mrs. Kleng denounced Sweeper and his companion for their treachery.

"My husband planned this whole reservoir set-up," she declared, "and now you think you're going to rob him! He's the one who got the syndicate to promise the backing and what have you done, but—"

"I've done plenty!" Sweeper cut in. "And if it weren't for my brains, this whole operation would have been sunk!"

The woman snorted contemptuously. "Brains! You're so stupid you left the front door unlocked while you robbed the safe!"

Green spoke up excitedly, "We couldn't help it. The lock was jammed!"

"Pipe down!" ordered Sweeper. "Somebody'll hear you!"

After that the voices fell and the boys could catch only a sharp word now and then. Suddenly the front door opened and the Hardys whirled to see Chief Collig with Chet.

Quietly the two walked to Frank and Joe. "Reinforcements coming," the chief said softly. "The men still in there?"

Frank nodded. "Mrs. Kleng's with them, and they didn't seem too happy to see her." Briefly, he whispered what he and Joe had overheard.

Chief Collig nodded, then walked past the boys to the office. With one quick movement, he threw open the door. "All right, lady," he said. "Step aside."

Mrs. Kleng whirled around with a startled look. "What's the idea?" she asked.

"You're all under arrest!" the chief announced gruffly.

Sweeper saw the boys and snarled. Green stood gasping like a hooked fish.

"You can't arrest me!" Mrs. Kleng's voice rose shrilly. "My husband owns this shop! I came here for some money he asked me to get for him and found these two crooks"—she pointed a bony finger at Sweeper and Green—"breaking into the safe! They're the guilty ones!"

Collig was not impressed. "I'm holding you as a material witness."

Mrs. Kleng flashed him a bitter look. "Do what you want. I won't talk."

The chief produced a pair of handcuffs and chained the two men together.

"Sweeper," said Frank, "where's Dr. Foster?"

"I don't know what you're talking about," the tall man replied.

"You'd better tell us," Joe said sharply.

Sweeper raised his brows. "Take it easy, boy. You don't know who I am. I'll be out of this jam before daylight."

"You're Timothy Kimball Jr.," said Joe, "and this is one time your father can't help you."

The thief stared at Joe. "You think you're pretty smart, figuring that out."

"You'd be wise to cooperate, Kimball," said the chief. "Where's that hideout?"

Sweeper's lips tightened. "I'm telling nothing," he said. "And neither is Green, if he knows what's good for him."

The small man gulped. " 'Course not, Sweeper. I won't talk."

Sweeper gave the Hardys a twisted smile. "It's all up to you, boys," he said. "Good luck!"

Flanked by the boys, the chief marched his three prisoners to the door, where a squad car had pulled up.

"This takes care of some of the crooks," Joe said, grinning. "Now for the others!"

CHAPTER XVIII

The Secret Tunnel

DAYLIGHT was breaking over Skull Mountain when Frank and Joe climbed to the top of the narrow trail. Bob and Dick greeted them on the ridge.

The boys unslung the gas masks from their shoulders and handed one to each of the engineers, keeping a mask apiece for themselves. All had canteens and flashlights.

"Where's Chet?" asked Dick.

"Still in the sack," Joe replied with a grin. "He's coming later in his jalopy."

"See your dad?" Bob questioned them, looping the strap of his mask around his neck.

"No," said Frank. He quickly told all that had happened the night before.

"Did you tell the police about the tunnel that you think goes to the gang's hideout?" Bob asked.

"Yes," replied Frank, "and while we were at

Chief Collig's office last night, he called Dad in Chicago. We reported all we'd discovered so far, and it was decided to round up the gang here tomorrow."

Joe explained that Mr. Hardy was ready to arrest the members of the syndicate in Chicago, but figured he might need one more day.

"In the meantime," Frank put in, "he wants us to locate the cavern and any tunnels that go to it. We're to sketch the layout for the police, so they can cut off all avenues of escape."

Bob gave a low whistle. "If one of the gang catches sight of you, it could wreck the whole operation."

"To say nothing of what they'd do to you if they nab you," Dick added.

"It'll be touchy," Frank agreed with a grin.

"We'll be glad to help you," said Bob.

Dick nodded. "Just say what you want us to do."

"Thanks," said Frank. "First let's see if there's water in the channel. After that, we'll tackle the right-hand branch of the tunnel."

A moment later the rectangular slab of rock had been removed and the crevice exposed.

Joe slid into the fissure, then Bob and Dick followed. Frank came last, and using the handhold, pulled the rock over the opening. The Hardys turned on their lights and crawled single file into the low-roofed tunnel ahead.

The four worked their way downward on their hands and knees. After a while they were able to walk erect. When they reached the fork, Joe paused. For a few minutes the boys listened for a sound from the right-hand shaft.

"You think the gang is down there now?" Bob asked quietly.

"Could be," Frank replied. "We'd better be quiet. No telling how sound carries in these passages."

Walking softly, the boys descended the tunnel which led to the underground stream. As they drew closer, the Hardys realized there was no sound of rushing water. Soon the floor leveled off, and the four saw the small landing ahead. They hastened to the edge and Frank shone his light downward. The floor below was damp, and tiny pools of water sparkled in the light. But the stream they had seen the night before was gone!

"That proves it!" Frank declared, his eyes shining. "This is the tunnel which runs from the reservoir!"

Bob nodded. "There's no doubt of that now," he said slowly. He stared down at the empty channel. "There can be only one explanation why the water flows through at night and not during the day," he added. "And that's a lock! It's probably close to the mouth of the tunnel."

Dick grinned. "All we have to do now," he pointed out, "is what we've been trying to do all along—locate the entrance to the channel and close it!"

"Maybe we could just block it off here," Joe suggested.

Bob shook his head. "We couldn't be sure the block would hold in this place."

Joe played his flashlight beam down on a jagged gap in the rock wall across the shaft.

"As long as the water's dammed up during the day," he said hopefully, "one of us might be able to crawl through that opening and along the tunnel to the mouth!"

"Nothing doing!" Frank told his brother. "That hole is too small as it is, and the passage may get a lot smaller as it goes along!"

"Frank's right, Joe," Bob said. "It could be suicide! We'll just have to keep hunting for the mouth of the tunnel until we find it."

Joe chuckled. "If the roundup comes off tomorrow, you won't have to look any more. We'll get the information from the gang."

But as the boys climbed up the tunnel again, the Hardys thought seriously of the next day. As seasoned detectives, they knew better than to be overconfident.

When the four reached the fork, they stopped. Dick nodded toward the other branch of the tunnel. "Ready for a look-see?" he asked softly.

"Wait," said Frank. "I think it would be wise

to cover ourselves. Chet should be at the camp by now. We'll go down and tell him what we're doing. If we don't come back in a reasonable time, he can go for help."

The others agreed and they continued to the top of the mountain. After crawling out of the crevice, they placed the stone over it and hurried down the mountain.

When they reached the shack, they found Chet pouring himself a glass of milk.

"Make it five glasses," Dick said, "and we'll tell you our news."

Joe spoke up. "Chet, my boy, we have a job for you."

His plump friend looked up warily. "Take it easy," he said. "I'm not over yesterday's job yet."

"All you need is a wrist watch," Frank said. "You check around four o'clock this afternoon and if we aren't back by then, you head for the nearest telephone and inform Chief Collig."

Joe explained what the day's plan was and quickly told Chet how to reach the entrance to the tunnels so that he could lead the police if necessary.

"Meanwhile, maybe you could help the sounding crew," Bob said. "The electronic equipment should be here in a few hours."

"Okay," said Chet. "That sounds safe enough."

"I'd like to give the crew instructions before

we head back to the summit," said Bob, and the others walked down toward the men's quarters with him.

Going down the slope of the reservoir, Frank noted that the hard ground underfoot was covered with the stumps of bramble bushes. Nearby was the large patch of heavy shrubbery left by the clearing crew. The water had risen as usual, covering part of the bushes. Frank paused and gazed at them thoughtfully.

"No use looking at that," Dick said gloomily. "We've prodded it a thousand times, I guess. There's nothing but solid rock underneath."

"I'll bet it's brambles," said Frank, "like the rest of the stuff that was cut down around here."

"So what?" said Chet. "With solid rock underneath there can't be a tunnel."

But Frank was already striding across the slope. "I'm going to have another look," he called back.

As the others followed, they saw Frank reach the shrubs and break off a piece.

When Joe trotted up, his brother held out the twig. "Brambles."

The Hardys peered into the thorny bushes. "They're not growing as close to the ground as they look," Joe remarked. "We could crawl in underneath and check that stone, if you want to."

"It'll be a scratchy job," Frank said, "but I think we'd better."

He stooped and crept into an opening at the

base of the bushes. Joe followed. To their surprise, if they kept low, the branches barely touched them.

Inside the bramble patch it was dim, but sunlight filtered through and dappled the steep slope. A foot or so below them, amid the dark branches, the water lapped softly. Near the center of the bushes, they came to a huge slab of rock resting against the hillside with its base hidden in the water.

Suddenly Frank gripped his brother's arm and pointed to the top edge of the rock. A narrow opening lay just above it!

Quick examination showed other gaps between the slab and the hill. *Behind the rock was an opening!*

"The tunnel!" exclaimed Frank. "This must be it!"

"But how do you get in?"

The brothers pulled hard at the edge of the slab. Suddenly, with a swish of the water, the big stone pivoted out about a foot.

Hearts pounding, the boys gazed into a dark tunnel with water gleaming on the bottom.

Joe gave a low two-toned whistle which Chet knew as a signal and in a few minutes the others stood with the Hardys at the mouth of the channel.

Bob and Dick could hardly keep from shouting for joy, but all remained silent.

They shone their lights into the narrow opening and saw that the gap behind the stone was roughly twelve feet high by six feet wide. Four feet above their heads was a narrow wooden catwalk built on supports which rested on the tunnel bottom. Just inside the entrance was a crude set of wooden rungs leading up to the catwalk.

Suddenly from deep inside the mountain came a high-pitched cry for help. The boys froze as it quavered and died. Once more it came. Then silence. The listeners exchanged anxious looks. Had it been Dr. Foster?

Frank's eyes narrowed with decision. "Chet," he said crisply, "you drive to the nearest phone and call Chief Collig. Tell him the rescue won't wait till tomorrow. We'll meet you and the police at the shack in two hours."

"Take the convertible," put in Joe.

"Meanwhile we'll case the layout," said Frank, "the way Dad asked us to."

"Okay," said Chet, and promptly started crawling out of the shrubbery. "Good luck," he called back hoarsely as the others began climbing the ladder to the catwalk.

They saw that the side walls of the tunnel were made of shale, clay, and limestone. The dim light coming through the narrow opening behind them enabled the four explorers to see for a distance of several feet. But directly ahead the tunnel turned sharply and was lost in darkness.

The boys waited on the catwalk while Bob, who was last, reached out and easily pulled the big stone shut again. "It's balanced on a pivot," he thought.

Then they flicked on their flashlights and cautiously followed Joe, who was in the lead.

At the first turn he stopped. "Don't need lights. Lanterns ahead," he whispered to Frank, who passed the information down the line.

Walking under the flickering oil lanterns which had been strung along the passage, the boys felt keenly the danger of their position. Suppose someone came toward them around the next bend or into the tunnel from behind? There was no place to hide!

Hearts pounding, they rounded the second bend and stopped. "The lock!" Dick whispered.

Before them was a crude wooden structure nearly as high as the catwalk. It had two doorlike wings made of planks which met in the center. When the wings were closed, as they were now, the water was impounded. Behind the lock, the ditch was dry.

"There's the gadget that operates it," Bob whispered. He indicated an iron wheel at the side of the tunnel. It resembled the brake wheel of a railway freight car.

The four continued quietly along the wooden

walk. Suddenly, when about to turn another bend, they heard footsteps approaching. The searchers stopped dead.

"Into the ditch!" Frank exclaimed softly, and swung himself down into the channel. Noiselessly the other three did the same. They flattened themselves against the rock wall under the catwalk. The footsteps came nearer and passed overhead.

The boys peered out and saw the man's back in the light of a lantern. *Sailor Hawkins!* Briefly he inspected the lock, then returned along the catwalk. The four lifted themselves out of the sluiceway as soon as the old seaman had disappeared.

"That cavern where the men hide out can't be far ahead!" Frank whispered excitedly.

He and his companions moved forward again. In a few moments they came to a small cave on the left. Joe poked his head in for a look around, but withdrew it with a start.

"Skulls!" he whispered. "The hermit's supply room!"

Finally the boys and the engineers reached a cleft in the rock wall of the passage. Its floor, starting on a level with the catwalk, sloped upward for several feet. Then the crack expanded into a deep cavern, dimly lighted by lanterns.

From the darkness of the cleft, the four could

see another fissure which slanted upward into the far wall of the big chamber.

Frank pointed to it. "That shaft must be the one which leads to the fork," he whispered. On one side of it was a kiln and on the other a workbench. Stacked against the wall were boxes of supplies and across the chamber was a group of cots.

"Quiet!" Bob warned. "There's a man!"

From an opening in the right wall strode Sailor Hawkins. He was carrying a plank, which he took to the bench and began sawing. The blade bit into the wood with swift, efficient strokes, and the boys observed that the seaman was cutting a board the same length and width as the planks in the lock.

"I'll bet Hawkins built the lock," Bob whispered.

"Look!" Frank whispered. "Here comes the hermit!"

The gaunt figure was staggering down the shaft from the mountaintop, his arms laden with split cordwood. He dropped the wood on the floor and walked to one corner of the room, where he sat on a box and leaned against the rock wall.

"Look!" Joe whispered, and pointed to the opening from which Hawkins had come.

A frail, slightly stooped man with white hair

stood there uncertainly. Then he walked to the kiln, opened the oven, took out something and examined it. Beside the kiln stood a wheelbarrow, heaped with what looked like mud.

The hermit stood up and approached the old man in a deferential manner.

"That must be Dr. Foster!" Frank said in an excited whisper.

Joe nodded. "What's he doing?" he asked.

Frank shook his head, and Bob whispered back, "I don't know, but it looks as if he's testing something in the kiln—maybe that mud."

"Perhaps the gang believes there are mineral deposits in the valley," Frank said softly. "No wonder they don't want the water to rise there."

"Think Foster is a member of the gang?" Dick asked.

"I doubt it," Frank replied, keeping his voice down. "He doesn't look like the sort of man who would willingly get involved in anything crooked."

The fire door below the kiln had been opened, and the man of the mountain was stoking it with wood. A cloud of smoke poured from the galvanized-iron stack which led from the kiln into the shaftway beyond.

"There's the source of the mysterious smoke!" Joe whispered.

Suddenly two men walked into the cavern from the side opening. One, stocky and surly-looking, had red hair. The other, who was smaller, wore a rumpled business suit spotted with clay.

Frank started. "The first man is Kleng!" he muttered to Bob and Dick. "The other is the stranger who was with Kleng and Sweeper the night they set me adrift!"

The two men joined Dr. Foster and stared at the kiln. "What about it?" the stranger said impatiently. "Is it cesium?"

Dr. Foster turned to the man fearfully. "I've told you, Mr. Stoper," he began, "I need more time to make the—"

"Time!" Stoper barked. "You want me to knock you down again? Nobody hears you when you yell, you know," he added with an ugly smile. He stubbed his finger into the scientist's chest. "I want results—and fast! Get it?"

"Take it easy," Kleng protested. "We need the old man."

"I gave you four days to produce results," Stoper said. "You've got till midnight tomorrow. After that, the syndicate needs *nobody*. They pull out." His eyes narrowed coldly. "They'll make it rough on you, Kleng, for wasting their time."

The plumber's face glistened with sweat. "We're doing the best we can."

Stoper looked at his watch. "Where are Sweeper and Green? Why aren't they back?"

"I don't know. Yesterday they had errands to

do. This morning they were to go to my house and get some money from my wife. They should have been here an hour ago."

Stoper paced nervously. "I don't like it. Maybe I ought to close this operation right now. Finish off the old man and—"

"No, no, Ben!" Kleng said. "Wait till tomorrow."

The hidden watchers barely breathed as Stoper scowled, considering what to do. Finally he said, "Okay—one more day. Cesium's worth it."

Cesium! Ben! The Hardys exchanged knowing glances. The parts of their puzzle were beginning to form a clear picture. Cesium was the precious metal the gang hoped to extract from the ore in the valley. The boys knew it was important in the production of photoelectric cells and transistors. And Stoper was Ben, the sender of the telegram Kleng had received.

"We'd better get back," Frank whispered.

The four watchers slipped noiselessly from their hiding place and started back along the catwalk. As they rounded the first turn, they stopped short, too startled to speak! Striding toward them was the stranger who had helped Hawkins carry the groceries! Before the boys could move, a revolver gleamed in his hand.

"All right," he said harshly. "Back you go!"

CHAPTER XIX

A Surprising Explanation

KLENG AND Ben Stoper stared as the Hardy boys and the engineers were herded into the cavern.

"Where'd you find them?" Stoper demanded of the man who held the gun.

"Just outside—on the catwalk," he replied.

Kleng's face hardened. "How'd you locate the tunnel?" he barked.

"We knew it was hidden by brambles," Joe replied. As he held the men's attention with the story of the twig on the barrel stave, Frank quietly sized up the situation.

The man of the mountain was gone, but a hard-faced man lounged beside the crevice which led to the mountaintop. It was the fellow who had thrown the can into the surf. Dr. Foster stood trembling by the kiln, plainly too frail to help the boys.

"Four of them, and four of us," Frank figured, "and one is armed—maybe the others." He decided it would be best to stall and wait for Chet to arrive with the police. "When he doesn't find us at the shack, he'll lead them here," Frank thought.

As Joe finished talking, Stoper turned to Kleng with a sneer. "These kids are smarter than you and your whole bunch of bunglers."

Kleng's face grew red. "Don't worry. Nobody else'll find that opening!"

"Unless they told somebody where it is," Stoper said smoothly. Then he barked at Frank, "Where's that fat kid?"

"Yeah," said a hoarse voice. It was the man lounging at the crevice. "Maybe he's running for the cops right this minute. Want me to try to head him off?"

"Hold it, Hank," Stoper ordered, and turned to the man with the revolver. "Did you let one get away, Fox?" he asked sarcastically.

The man's eyes flashed. "You think you're a big wheel from Chicago, Stoper, but all you've done so far is talk. How'd you like to sit all night on the mountain with a rifle and—"

"Don't give me that!" Stoper broke in. "Where were you when the Hardys dropped their floats in the reservoir?"

Fox blustered. "We didn't think anybody would go down there that night. The hermit reported that the engineers had left the mountain!"

"Shut up you two!" barked Kleng. "You're wasting time!" He poked Joe in the chest. "You—where's the fat boy?"

"He's not on the mountain," Joe replied.

"Then forget him," Kleng said to his companions. He signaled Fox, who gave Bob a push.

"March!" The four were herded into the small dimly lighted rock chamber which adjoined the cavern. They were ordered to lie down on the damp floor. Their hands and feet were securely tied, then the men left.

The minutes dragged on. The Hardys and the engineers discussed their situation, then subsided into worried silence, each occupied with his own thoughts. What were Kleng's plans for them? Suppose he acted before Chet and the police arrived? One thing was certain: Kleng would not allow them to go free and expose him and his gang.

Suddenly the prisoners heard footsteps and a moment later Hawkins appeared, thrusting Dr. Foster before him. Directing the scientist to lie on the floor, the sailor quickly tied his hands and feet.

As soon as Hawkins clomped out of the room, Frank turned to the white-haired man. He appeared to be near the breaking point. "What happened?"

The scientist grimaced. "Stoper would wait no longer. They forced me to talk. I had to tell them there was no cesium in the ore they brought me to test. Now they will get rid of all of us."

His voice quavered. "No doubt you're all wondering why I'm mixed up with those men. This is the story."

Several years ago, he told them, before Tarnack Dam had been blueprinted, he had prospected for cesium on Skull Mountain. He had read the geological theory of the subterranean passage but thought it fanciful. One day, however, while poking along the hillside, then densely forested, he had come upon the mouth of the channel.

"I explored the tunnel with great excitement," the scientist said, "and discovered deposits of ore which contained cesium."

He coughed, chilled by the damp floor, then continued. "Deep inside the mountain, I found the cavern, and the cleft running clear to the top of the ridge! Gentlemen, what awe I felt when I saw this ancient natural wonder!" He paused, remembering the experience.

"How do Kleng and Stoper fit into this?" Joe asked.

Kleng, Dr. Foster explained, had been recommended to him as a man who could raise money to work the deposits in the tunnel. The scientist had told the plumber he was not positive that

Their hands and feet were securely tied

there was enough cesium to make it worth mining, but he wanted to test more of the ore and find out.

Kleng had been tremendously interested in the project, and had persuaded Dr. Foster to show him the tunnel. But the plumber had failed to raise the money, and plans for testing the deposits had to be abandoned.

"Then, about five weeks ago," the scientist went on, "I received a telegram from Kleng. He told me a group of men had agreed to put up the money for the project, and permission to mine the tunnel had been granted by the Coastal Power and Light Company. I know now that was a lie. Kleng insisted that I come to Bayport at once."

Dr. Foster's voice became bitter. "When I got here, I found that I was not only to analyze ore from the tunnel, but also some from the slopes of the reservoir. Kleng's men brought it in at night and camouflaged their digging with low shrubs."

"The rats!" Bob said. "To keep the valley clear to mine the cesium, Kleng had to keep the reservoir from filling up."

"Yes," said Dr. Foster. "I saw what their scheme was. Then I discovered I was a prisoner! I knew they would dispose of me as soon as the tests were finished, so I insisted they bring me a kiln."

The boys looked puzzled and Dr. Foster explained. "The gang thought it was necessary for the tests. Of course it was not. I used the kiln to stall for time and make smoke, which I hoped someone would see and investigate."

"But how could the gang hope to get away with the mining operation?" Dick asked, puzzled.

"The Chicago syndicate is powerful," the scientist said. "They control an engineering company which was to mine the ore under the pretense of cutting away the reservoir banks to solve the escaping water problem. Stoper said this firm would have no trouble getting the job from the Coastal Power and Light Company."

"Did Hawkins build the lock?" Frank asked.

Dr. Foster nodded. "The old sailor was incensed at the prospect of losing his home because of the water project, and Kleng found him a willing ally in his scheme to divert the water to the sea."

"Does Potato Annie fit into the picture?" asked Bob.

Dr. Foster said that she had helped the gang for the same reason, supplying them with vegetables from her garden.

"What about the shaggy old guy?" Frank asked.

"Yes," Joe said grimly. "We've plenty of things to settle with him!"

Dr. Foster coughed gently. "I can well imagine how you feel about Tom Darby," he said, "but I

hope you won't hold him responsible for all of
his actions. He's devoted to me, and terrified of
the others. Kleng threatened to send him back
to the county poor farm if he did not obey orders.
Otherwise, I'm sure he would have helped me
escape."

"What do you know about him?" Dick asked.

Tom Darby, the scientist said, had run away
from the county poor farm in the adjoining state
and ever since had been living like a hermit.

"I met Tom on my first trip to Skull Mountain," Dr. Foster declared. "He was half starved
and nearly naked. But when I tried to help him,
he ran away.

"Later, I won the old fellow's confidence, and
from then on, Tom couldn't do enough for me.
When I returned this summer, he was still here.
He lived in the tunnel and had been subsisting
pretty much on vegetables which he sneaked from
Annie's garden. She was afraid of him, but Hawkins and the other squatters gave him regular
handouts."

Dr. Foster's eyes twinkled. "It was Tom's idea
to frighten you with skulls. Kleng told Tom anything he did to scare you away from the mountain
would be of great help to me!"

"Tom must think an awful lot of you, sir," Joe
said ruefully. "He did his best to get rid of us!"

Dick interrupted. "Smashed equipment, boulders, an explosion, a fire—"

"Sweeper supplied Tom with the dynamite," the scientist said, "but the gang was angry because he did not plant it close enough to really hurt you. Then Kleng took over and set fire to your shack. Tom Darby wouldn't stoop to such things. He was sorry about the landslide, for he only meant to frighten you with the boulder." Dr. Foster sighed. "If we get out of here alive, I will take Tom with me. My brother has a large estate where the poor fellow can have a cottage to himself and be well taken care of."

The scientist stopped speaking, for at that moment Kleng came in carrying a lantern. He looked around at them with a thin smile. "Foster's probably told you our job is finished," he said harshly. "But before we leave, I'm going to fix it so you won't be able to tell your story to the cops."

Suddenly he shouted over his shoulder, "Hawkins! Get the dynamite!"

The prisoners stiffened and a cold chill ran down Frank's spine.

Kleng's voice grew silky. "That's right, fellows. Hawkins is going to dynamite the mouth of the tunnel and close it up. You'll be buried alive!"

CHAPTER XX

Smoked Out

HORRIFIED at the threat, the prisoners stared at one another, speechless. Kleng had left the room. They could hear him in the adjoining cavern instructing Hawkins in the use of the dynamite.

Frank thought of the crevice. "We still have a chance!" he whispered to the others. "If we can break out of these ropes, we'll climb the shaft and escape through the top of the mountain!"

But Kleng's next words stifled that hope. "After you've blasted the mouth of the tunnel," he told Hawkins, "come back here and set off another charge to plug the shaft. That'll seal everything nice and tight."

"Aye, cap'n," the sailor replied. "But how are we to get away?"

"Up the shaft, you fool. Stoper, Hank, Fox, and I will go ahead while you blow the tunnel. You'll follow up this shaft and then blast it. Now get going."

The prisoners heard the sailor's footsteps recede. Then there was silence. Frantically they struggled with their bonds. They rolled close to one another, their fingers tearing at each other's ropes, but the strands were wet from the damp floor and resisted their attempts to untie them.

"There must be some way out of this!" Bob said desperately.

He lifted his wrists to a jagged edge of rock and tried to saw through the binding hemp, but soon gave up, exhausted.

At that moment Tom Darby slipped into the small chamber, his arms piled with firewood. He stared at the prisoners, then dropped his load of wood and knelt beside Dr. Foster.

"Tom!" the scientist exclaimed. "Hurry, Tom! Untie me!"

The shaggy-haired man cast a terrified glance over his shoulder, then began fumbling with the rope. Frank and Joe and the two engineers looked on, hardly daring to breathe.

Suddenly a stocky figure appeared in the opening—Kleng! As the boys cried a warning, he grabbed a piece of firewood and struck the hermit on the head. The old man slumped to the floor, unconscious!

Kleng glanced at the rope which secured the scientist's wrists. He gave a satisfied grunt, then went out. A moment later the prisoners heard the four men start up the shaft toward the top of the mountain.

"There they go," Dick said tensely. "Pretty soon Hawkins will follow them, and then—" Everyone knew what he meant.

Suddenly Joe thought of his water canteen. He rolled his body toward the hermit and sat up. Twisting his bound wrists, he managed to unscrew the cap of the canteen on his hip. He tilted the flask so that water splashed on Darby's face.

The hermit stirred. His eyelids fluttered weakly. Joe splashed the bearded face again. The hermit looked at him, dazed.

"You've done it, Joe!" Frank exclaimed excitedly.

Dick turned to the scientist. "Hurry, Dr. Foster! Make Tom untie these ropes!"

Within a few minutes the hermit had freed Dr. Foster's hands and feet. Then the two men set to work on the others. Soon all the prisoners stood free.

"Come on, Dick!" Bob urged. "We must stop Hawkins before he seals the tunnel opening!"

"I'm with you!" his assistant replied. They raced through the cavern and into the lantern-lighted tunnel.

"We'll follow Kleng and Stoper!" Joe yelled after them. He ran to the shaft which sloped toward the mountaintop. "Come on, Frank!"

"Joe—wait! That's no good! Fox has a gun!"

"But we can't let them get away!"

"They won't!" Frank signaled to Dr. Foster and Tom Darby to follow him and went quickly to the kiln. Pointing toward the pile of green firewood, he said, "Feed the fire and get up plenty of smoke. We'll give 'em a taste of their own medicine!"

"Great!" exclaimed Joe, then snapped his fingers. "Ropes!" He dashed to the side chamber, picked up the discarded bonds, and stuffed them in his pockets.

The Hardys slipped on the gas masks which were still slung over their shoulders, and started up the shaft after the four men. The passage was smooth and wide, so that they quickly reached the fork, and hurried onto the low-roofed tunnel. By the time they had crawled halfway up it, the air was filling with smoke and they could hear coughing and strangled cries for help. In a few minutes their flashlights revealed the men clutching at their throats as they gasped for breath.

Helpless, the four were dragged by the Hardys up through the tunnel and out the opening in the mountaintop. After disarming the men and tying them up, the boys took off the gas masks. It was several minutes before any of the rescued men could speak. Then Kleng glared at his captors. "You!" he sputtered.

"Look who's coming!" Frank exclaimed.

Climbing the mountainside were Bob and Dick. A few steps behind them came Chet Morton, Fenton Hardy, and several policemen.

"Dad!" Frank exclaimed in delight as the party reached the top of the trail. "When did you get back?"

"Not long ago," Mr. Hardy said, and grinned when he saw the captured men. "Too late for the action, though!" He told them that he had wound up the Chicago end of the case sooner than he had expected and had been in Chief Collig's office when Chet's call came.

"When Dick and I got to the mouth of the tunnel," Bob spoke up, "your dad already had Hawkins in handcuffs!"

"I left him at the foot of the hill in care of the police," Mr. Hardy explained. "Several officers went into the cavern to escort Dr. Foster and the hermit out." The detective turned to Kleng and Stoper. "The law especially wants you two," he told them, "for holding Dr. Foster against his will. Your pals are already in jail!"

The four men glowered but said nothing. The police hauled them to their feet and marched them down the trail.

Chet grimaced. "I'm glad that's all over!"

Fenton Hardy laughed and threw his arm around the boy. "Chet, you did your part well!"

"You bet he did!" Frank said sincerely.

Joe sighed. "Well, I guess this winds up the mystery!"

"Don't take it so hard," Frank comforted him with a grin. "Another one will turn up soon!"

Although he did not realize it at the time, Frank was speaking the truth. The Hardy boys were closer than they knew to the mystery connected with *The Sign of the Crooked Arrow*.

Now, standing on the crest of Skull Mountain, the young detectives, their father, and their friends stared down Tarnack Valley. Soon the mouth of the prehistoric tunnel would be walled up forever. Then the thin sheet of water which now covered the valley would become a deep lake.

Bob and Dick smiled happily as they visualized it, while Frank and Joe exchanged grins.

"Guess we're thinking the same thing," said Frank.

"We sure are," Joe replied. "Now we'll have plenty of water in the swimming pool!"